Face of a Stranger

Face of a Stranger

a novel

Yoji Yamaguchi

HarperCollinsPublishers

HarperCollins books may be purchased for educational, business, or sales promotional use. For information please write: Special Markets Department, HarperCollins Publishers, Inc., 10 East 53rd Street, New York, NY 10022.

FIRST EDITION

Designed by Nancy Singer

Library of Congress Cataloging-in-Publication Data

Yamaguchi, Yoji, 1963–
    Face of a stranger : a novel / Yoji Yamaguchi. — 1st ed.
        p.   cm.
    ISBN 0-06-017235-5
    I. Title.
    PS3575.A424F33   1995
    813'.54—dc20   95-11471

95 96 97 98 99 ❖/HC 10 9 8 7 6 5 4 3 2 1

For my parents

What's here? The portrait of a blinking idiot

Presenting me a schedule. . . .

> —Shakespeare, *The Merchant of Venice*

one

Whores worked out of clapboard shacks in a place called China Alley—a misnomer, as there were no Chinese to be found. They had quit the town nearly a decade ago, after the Japanese, fresh off the boat and hungry for riches, underbid their hire for all the laborers' jobs and quickly laid claim to the entire immigrant quarter. But the name had been coined by Americans, and none of the Japanese felt inclined to quibble over those ramshackle huts, so China Alley it remained.

Vain, handsome Takashi Arai sauntered down the dark row, scanning it as if searching for a woman in particular, though in truth he did not know one from the other. He had been to the quarter only once before, and could not remember which hut he had visited.

Prostitutes were a luxury he could

rarely afford. But he had won big at *fan-tan* at Kato's gambling den that night, an unusual occurrence (most nights he was fortunate to leave without owing the house). Moreover, he had just received his first paycheck from his new job—his twelfth in the last three years—working as a domestic for two elderly spinsters. His pockets full, his heart still racing from the thrill of winning (and several rounds of whiskey), Takashi wanted a woman.

He stopped to turn up the collar of his pea coat (a stolen memento of his brief stint on a cargo boat out of Alaska) against the chill air of the late autumn night. The unwelcome memory of his only previous visit came back to him. The woman—Wada, she called herself, or so he remembered—almost frightened him at first; she looked like a ghost. Her bones protruded visibly under her pasty white skin; her coarse, matted hair flew out in all directions; and her bloodshot eyes had the look of opium. She took his money, shed her dress, and flopped on the cot, waiting silently as he fumbled with his trousers. When he entered her, she lay so still that for a moment he thought she had fallen asleep—until she coughed, violently and loudly in his ear, causing her loins to convulse and unceremoniously jettison his member.

"Lousy senpu," he muttered to the empty alley, his tumescence beginning to ebb.

In spite of himself, he held out his arms and inspected his clothes. A pale crescent of his once-white, now wheat-colored shirt peeked out through a tear in the armpit of his coat. His shoes were badly scuffed, and the big toe of his left foot was beginning to insinuate itself through the worn leather. His

Yoji Yamaguchi

trousers were wrinkled and threadbare, nearly gauzelike in places. What was he, after all, but a *buranke katsugi*, a blanket-carrying migrant worker, and now, of all things, a *houseboy*?

The scion of a successful provincial merchant family who made their fortune in sake, as a boy Takashi had been expelled by every private school in their prefecture. But his father was not so stern as to banish his eldest son halfway across the world simply for youthful mischief. Unfortunately, Takashi's scandalous conduct ruined a lucrative match Mr. Arai had spent years trying to arrange, one between Takashi and the daughter and only child of a much wealthier merchant family all the way from Tokyo; the marriage would have made Takashi heir to his in-laws, thereby linking the two families.

He was startled out of his reverie by a shriek. A woman burst out of one of the shacks and threw herself at him, babbling incoherently. She was a round-faced young girl, no older than sixteen, with droopy, hooded eyelids and a boy's body. The red, tasseled dress was a size too large and made her look like a grotesque, shrunken doll. "It's you, it's you, you're finally here. Where have you been? Where have you been?" she sobbed over and over.

Takashi could only stammer "What? What?"

"Oh, that terrible man—Saigo, he called himself—he said you were ill and couldn't come, and he would take me to you. Why weren't you there? Now look what's become of me." She sniffled.

Abruptly she smiled. "Oh, how lucky I was to be looking out the window just as you were walking by!" Then, just as quickly,

Face of a Stranger

her countenance darkened. "And what do you think you're doing here?" she demanded sharply.

"I don't understand. I think . . . there's been a mistake."

She shoved him in the chest. "Yes, it was my mistake. I never should have married you! What kind of husband are you, bringing me all the way to America, then leaving me stranded?"

"Husband?"

A man approached. "Nan da yo? I was here first. You're gonna hafta wait your turn, boy," he growled.

Even though he was a foot shorter than Takashi, and looked about twice his age, his grizzled face and thick, hamlike arms were enough to convince Takashi not to mess with him.

The man grabbed the woman by the arm. "C'mon, girl. Back to work."

"No, this is my husband and I'm not your girl! You can't use me anymore." She struggled to free her arm.

He roared with laughter. "This is your wife, boy? What's the matter, ain't you got a job of your own?"

"No. I mean, she's not . . . I don't know . . . ah, there's been a mistake."

The woman glared at him, then slapped him across the face. "Coward! Are you afraid of this pig? I thought you were a war hero. You said in your letter that you killed Russians with your bare hands."

The short burly man cocked his head back and folded his arms. Takashi started walking. "I have to go."

The man hoisted the woman on his shoulder. "C'mon, I've had enough of this. Time to earn your money."

4

Takashi walked away. He could hear behind him the woman's shrill, panicked voice, calling him by someone else's name, with the man's harsh laughter booming in the background. "Shuji-san! Shuji-san! Matte! Wait! Come back! I'm your wife, you can't leave me like this!" Then he heard a door slam and all was quiet again. His face burning with embarrassment, his ardor shriveled like a dried-up weed, he fled the alley in a panic.

What a nuisance, he thought as he walked hurriedly, though without direction, digging his hands into his pockets: a face confused, a name misplaced, and suddenly another man's life—his accumulation of debts, obligations, affections, and grievances—foisted on him.

Takashi wanted to believe that the woman was simply myopic, drunk, or mad, but he knew better. She was not the first to mistake him. There were at least a dozen others before her, housewives who spotted him on the street and stopped dead in their tracks to gape at him in a most indecorous fashion.

Other men attributed this phenomenon to Takashi's fine-boned, elegant face. It was a running joke among the bachelors and a sore point for the husbands; they called him Kao-sama, Master Face, the man who entranced women just by looking at them.

But vain as he was, Takashi knew there was nothing magical about his face. The way each of the women had looked at him—the contorted shock of recognition, the pained grimace clouding over, and then the black, icy bitterness—told him everything. It had to be the picture.

5

Three years before when the old man Kori offered Takashi thirty bucks for a photo of him and even agreed to pay the photographer, Takashi never foresaw his present dilemma. Kori told him that he had been looking for a picture bride from Japan and saw the perfect woman. The old man spoke as if he were describing the visage of a goddess instead of a wallet-size photo of an anonymous woman tacked on the bulletin board in the dusty, ill-lit office of the labor boss who doubled as a marriage broker for his hard up, lonesome hires (and anyone else willing to fork up the requisite fees). He couldn't remember her name at that moment, but it sounded high-class.

Unfortunately, the boss told him no chance. While Kori could no doubt provide a handsome wedding gift and a more than adequate living for any woman, all the gold in America couldn't compensate for his age and (Kori chuckled sheepishly) his looks.

It made sense to Takashi; Kori's face reminded him of a grizzled old fox: a pointed nose, two tiny, deep-set eyes, and long, angular ears. The only unvulpine feature was his stark, shining head, which was shaped like a squash. Takashi pitied the old man trying to catch a young wife, forced to mask his face in order to do so.

Kori was not the only one. On the mainland, Issei men still outnumbered Issei women tenfold, and the only way to find a wife—short of making the exorbitant trip across the Pacific—was by sending a photo of one's self to prospective brides in Japan; the importance of appearances was utmost. Naturally,

Yoji Yamaguchi

the uncomeliest men—the hoary, hirsute, bald, fat, big-nosed, flat-faced—were at a disadvantage. So it was not uncommon for them to use outdated portraits that were taken at a more attractive age, or to hire a substitute. The families of the brides were not above this sort of practice, either.

Here Takashi hesitated. How many times had he seen a happy old man trailed by a crestfallen young woman who shuffled morosely and as deliberately as the tides so as not to overtake her doddering spouse? And how many times had he listened to a drunkard sitting beside him at the bar, mumbling a lament about his once-beautiful wife who had metamorphosed into a swarthy, basso-voiced giantess during the course of her trans-Pacific voyage?

Whatever misgivings Takashi may have had about engaging in this masquerade were quickly dashed by the wad of bills Kori flashed before him. The woman who marries a man who carries so much ready cash will be set for life, Takashi reasoned—I'd be doing her a favor.

The possibility that he might one day come face-to-face with the gulled Mrs. Kori never occurred to him. Nor did the off chance that Kori might be something other than a lovelorn old man in search of a wife.

What Takashi did know was that at least twelve women (thirteen, now) had landed at the new immigration station on Angel Island, expecting him to greet them on the San Francisco pier, and looked for his face among the eager, anxious men queuing on the dock, who were probably in turn searching for the right faces on the ferry's deck, glancing down at the photos in their

7

hands from time to time. Some of these women were taken home by jarringly homely husbands who bore no resemblance to their promises, and who were hard pressed, no doubt, to explain the vagaries of photographic mimesis or the transience of physical beauty. But some women, he now realized, were whisked off to saloons and whorehouses, where they were told, plain and simple, to work or die.

Takashi imagined an armada of immigrant ships steaming toward California, their steerage holds crammed with hopeful women, each of them clutching his photograph, eager to meet him but not him, some Taro, Jun, or Haruki wearing his face. He saw riots on the docks as the women, realizing they'd been had, fell on their hapless husbands, and the survivors, having just been told by their brides-to-be in no uncertain terms how wanting they were compared to the peerless man in the picture, set out, town by town, in search of this pretty despoiler, this dandy home wrecker, to tear him to messes in a jealous rage. And if they didn't get him, the women would, mobs of howling, teeth-baring women chasing him into the desert. A Society of Defrauded Brides would be founded, its membership in the thousands and spanning the entire West Coast, its sole mission to track down this treacherous Takashi Arai and bring him to justice.

Or, even worse—to bring him to marriage. Takashi shook his head as if to dissipate the vision that swelled in his mind: a wedding ceremony with a thousand brides and one groom.

One would expect that Takashi—who valued his looks more than anything—would be gratified at the willingness of so many women to cross an ocean to marry him. Instead, he felt like bait, thrown into the teeth of a hunting pack.

Takashi might not have given these women a second thought, if only he didn't keep running into them. After all, he had been taken in as much as they had. One need not have been a genius to figure out that the glibly self-effacing old man had been sharing—or, more likely, selling—Takashi's picture. That Kori would give this fellow Saigo the whore had mentioned—a lowly pimp, of all things—license to use his face was intolerable.

Drunken laughter escaped from one of the windows high above the street. He heard the whore again: *coward . . . what kind of husband are you?* His face flushed; his armpits felt clammy; his back prickled as if someone had stuffed cockleburs down his shirt. He clenched his fists and blurted out to the black silent night: "Isn't it natural for a wife to feel let down by her husband once they're married? What difference does it make whether it happens sooner or later?"

As if in response, a dog barked in the distance. Takashi, realizing he'd been talking to himself, picked up his pace.

After all, Takashi thought, these women came here just like everybody else—chasing after their own little fortune. So the siren's song turned into a shrill mocking laugh; so the chest of gold proved to be a pile of shit; in this these women were not alone.

Even after six years Takashi could still remember the words of that sign he saw in the window of the S. Ban Company, a labor export enterprise:

9

KITARE, NIHONJIN!

COME MERCHANTS! AMERICA IS A VERITABLE HUMAN PARADISE,
THE ICHI-BAN MINE IN THE WORLD! GOLD, SILVER, AND GEMS
ARE SCATTERED IN HER STREETS!

Now that was a pretty picture. But it didn't depict him stooped over picking lettuce under a scorching sun, or working as a houseboy for two churlish, dwarflike spinsters, the Warren twins Joan and Jane, and their irascible dog. This was the life Takashi found awaiting him in this veritable human paradise. Why should he feel bad for these picture brides who were just as gullible as him?

Takashi stopped and realized that he was back where he had started, not far from Nakagami's saloon. He hurried in that direction, eager for the solace of oblivion—not as sweet as a woman, perhaps, but cheaper and not so treacherous.

One of the women who worked on China Alley, Kikue, was the subject of much conjecture among her colleagues. She was older than most of the others, approaching her thirties, so it was said, and not especially beautiful. Fearfully thin, she had knobby shoulders and a long, sinewy neck. Wrinkles gathered around her eyes and mouth, and her dry, thin hair was already turning gray. Her long, slender hands might have been elegant once but were now coarse and leathery. Yet she attracted only the most reputable and prosperous Issei, local merchants, artisans, and farmers who were almost all of them well mannered and well

Yoji Yamaguchi

kept, with plenty of money in their pockets. The other women had to contend with the seamier elements—the gamblers, loan sharks, thugs, and indigents—coarse, unruly men, hardly fastidious about their appearances and even less so about such niceties as payment for services rendered. So it was a mixture of curiosity and envy that started tongues wagging.

One story had it that Kikue had been married once, until her husband caught her in bed with another man, whereupon he killed him and sold her off to a pimp, who promptly shipped her to America. Another version was that her father lost a wager to a labor contractor who had come to their town recruiting workers, and gave her away, as he was broke at the time.

The most widely accepted version was that a woman posing as a broker for a wealthy merchant gulled her parents into giving away their only daughter to marry his son in America, promising her first-class passage on a luxury liner, a mansion with a dozen maids waiting on them at all hours, two chauffeured cars, a sailboat, and a trip to Paris every summer. Had such gaudy enticements not been persuasion enough, she showed them the "son's" picture—a face, it was said, of such inestimable beauty that any woman would be happy to sail across an ocean in quest of its owner.

As one might expect of a woman in her situation, Kikue knew the secrets of many but volunteered few of her own. She knew, for instance, that Nakagami the saloon keeper had never been an army officer, as he claimed; in fact, he had been rejected by the draft board for his "obesity and general slovenliness." By the same token, Mr. Kunihara's father was neither a baron nor a former high-ranking *bakufu* official, as Kunihara was wont to boast in beery fits of nostalgia, but rather a low-ranking land-tax collector for the new federal government.

Perhaps because of the shady nature of her invitation to America, Kikue grew keen to all kinds of airs and pretenses. The offbeat pause in an affected accent; the effort behind a gesture; the seams in a constructed tale: in time, none of these escaped her eyes and ears. It was not hard for her to catch a man with his defenses wilted like the creases in yesterday's suit; since most of her customers tended to forget that she was sentient, they were all the more careless.

As she unraveled the lies that seemed to enwrap each new visitor like a tightly wound obi, she began to wonder if there was anyone to be trusted, accepted at face value.

Her single-room clapboard shack had a door on the side, an eighteen-inch portal braced with wooden bars facing the alleyway. A passerby could look inside and see her lying on a narrow barracks bed. A rickety nightstand was the only other furnishing; on it stood a kerosene lamp. A crude brazier was set in the floorboards in the middle of the room. The ragged remnant of a brown, fading tapestry drawn over the window meant she was entertaining.

Perchance hers was the only window open in the alley when something of a miracle occurred. Three unshaven men, field hands from the look of their clothes, staggered into her hut carrying a fourth, who was out cold and buck naked, stinking of liquor. They dumped his limp body facedown on her bed. One of them placed a neatly folded bundle of clothes on the floor.

12

"What's this? I don't do corpses," she protested.

The oldest of the trio, a stocky, leather-faced man with a pepper-gray beard, reached into his pocket and produced a wad of bills, thirty dollars in all. "Here," he said, holding out the money with an unsteady hand. "Humor us, please. We have an important favor to ask."

"What do you want? Who is this? What happened to him?"

The second man, a tall, sallow, bald-headed fellow, spoke up: "His name is Arai Takashi, an itinerant laborer. We met him this evening at a, er, social establishment, whereupon he declared to all present that he could out-drink the three of us combined. As this was, ah, something of an affront to us, we of course accepted his challenge. Although he is quite a, um, prodigious drinker, as you can see he was simply overwhelmed by our collective capacity." Discreetly, he suppressed a belch.

The older man spoke again: "He is quite a likeable sort, actually, a witty, lively fellow, and was truly enjoyable company at first. But once the whiskey began to loosen his tongue, I am afraid he became insufferably boastful. He seems to think he is blessed with greatness, and has rather inflated notions about his innate superiority to the rest of us, whom he thinks of as being merely run of the mill."

Kikue marveled at these scruffy-looking men and their refined (if somewhat slurred) way of speaking. She guessed that they were professionals or scholars back in Japan who were ruined financially and came to America in a wild attempt to reverse their fortunes. In this country, where a Japanese education meant nothing, it was not uncommon to find janitors fluent in classical Chinese, barbers with degrees in medicine.

"It is true." The bald one hiccupped. "We would like to think his brashness was from drink and youth. But there is more: as you can see, he is quite a handsome, virile-looking young man. Unfortunately, he seems to have allowed this whim of nature to go to his head. He fancies himself not only irresistible to all women, but entitled to their hearts' affections. When he began to recount his alleged numerous liaisons—sparing not a single detail—that was simply too much. If what he said was true, he has had more lovers at the age of twenty-four than most men could possibly hope to have in a lifetime."

The older man smiled and said: "Naturally, we are skeptical."

"He's full of shit, is what." The third man spoke up for the first time. He was much younger than the other two, roughly the same age as the man on the bed and nearly as drunk. He was short and pudgy and wanting a neck. In the dim light of the shack, his long, stringy hair and his pockmarked face gave off a greasy sheen. "He's all talk and no cock," he said, letting fly a fine spray of spittle.

The older man raged at him: "Damare! Mind your tongue!"

"What, she's just a whore," No Neck sneered, whereupon the bald man slapped him on the side of the head, nearly knocking him off his feet. "Please forgive our friend Isao," the bald man said, discreetly rubbing his fingers clean. "What you see here are the unfortunate side effects of Westernization on Japan's younger generations. Regrettably, the great liberal

14

thinkers, with all their emphasis on the individual, did not take into account the inherent baseness of mankind in general. To value freedom over civility absolutely can only lead to mischief." The older man nodded solemnly in assent. Kikue noticed that he was beginning to sway a bit.

"So what do you want?" she asked sharply. She was growing impatient with these long-winded fellows.

The older man said: "We would like you to determine for us whether our friend here is telling the truth about his experience in carnal matters."

"You mean . . . ?"

"So. We would like you to find out if he is still a virgin."

"But how could I tell?"

The bald one replied: "Because you are yourself a woman of, er, experience. We trust you will be able to spot a novice by his lack of, eh, dexterity and, um, endurance."

Isao snickered. The older man cuffed him in the ear, eliciting a yelp. Then he said: "As you can see, we have already taken the liberty of undressing him, so as to spare you the difficulty. Needless to say, we are indebted to you for your indulgence, and we hope we have not caused you too great an inconvenience."

Kikue said: "Wait. What am I supposed to do with him? He's dead to the world."

"We leave that to you," the bald one said as he turned to leave. He stopped at the door and added: "Mind you, we are not being malicious; we are not trying to humiliate him. We simply want to know the truth. That he feels compelled to lie to

15

us for the sake of self-aggrandizement is quite intolerable. Trust is precious, and not to be exploited. Friends should be honest with one another, wouldn't you agree?" With that, the three men bowed woodenly and said farewell, then staggered out of the shack, leaving Kikue with her comatose john.

The man rolled over onto his back, startling her, and began snoring, wheezing, grunting like a boar. His sleek, flawless skin, marred here and there by flushed, sanguine patches, shined like ceramic. He was tall and lean; his wiry muscles and sinews rippled, it seemed, with a barely dormant energy. His long, supple body reminded her of a rushing, white-water river as seen from a hilltop, his sex a dark, treacherous snag in midstream. His face was elegant, finely honed. Shorn of any sign of chubby boyishness, it retained the smooth softness of youth, and was highlighted by bold, slashing eyebrows, long, downlike lashes, a subtle peak of a nose, and a firm, graceful arc of a jaw. His cheeks were flushed from the liquor, giving him the look of wearing rouge.

Kikue stared at that sleeping, expressionless face, and gasped. Disbelief, anger, fear, humiliation, grief—all flooded into her mind at once. She bent over him, so low that her nose was inches from his; sour whiskey fumes poured into her nostrils.

She backed away, wrapping her arms around her body. The money the old man had given her fell from her hand. At that moment she trembled with the urge to suffocate the sleeper and drag his body outside for dogs to feed on.

Instead, she sat down heavily on the floor. She closed her eyes, unwilling to believe that there, lying on her bed, was the

16

promised son, the beautiful betrayer—the man who was to have been her husband.

Kikue sat before the brazier, her face illumined by the orange glow of the coals. Takashi Arai was still asleep, snoring to the heavens. As she stared at his motionless form, she could not help remembering everything she wanted to forget.

She should have known that all was amiss back at Yokohama, the minute she saw the ship bound for America—not a luxury liner as promised, but an old freighter, sitting low in the water and listing badly to port, its hull streaked with trails of rust. The marriage broker, a woman named Oshichi, had long disappeared; at the pier she had turned Kikue over to a man named Saigo. As soon as Kikue stepped on board, he whisked her below to the cargo hold.

"Why am I down here?" Kikue demanded, not yet fearful. "What happened to the cabin with the porthole that looks out on the sea?"

Saigo, an ugly man with a sharp, narrow face and a thick nose, laughed harshly. "They don't give cabins to whores."

Kikue remembered being stunned at the affront, thinking: *He doesn't even know me; how can he call me that?* Then she noticed something odd. "Where's my luggage . . . " She felt the boat moving beneath her feet; then she heard Saigo informing her that she had in fact been sold to his boss, the pimp Kato. "And if you don't work for him, after all the money he's paid for you, we'll kill you and then go back and kill your family," he warned.

Face of a Stranger

"Liar!" she shrieked, panicking. "Let me off the boat." She tried to run by him, but he blocked her path.

"Too late," he cackled. "We're already on our way. They're not going to turn this boat around just for you. 'Course, maybe if you gave the crew a quick one, they might think about it." He leered at her.

At that moment, Kikue felt as if she had been pushed off a cliff and was falling headlong, ever so slowly. As she sat in her hut recollecting, she closed her eyes and bowed her head in shame at how she buckled over and vomited without warning, then collapsed in a heap at Saigo's feet.

Better if I had clawed his eyes out, she thought.

Takashi's snoring grew louder. Kikue looked up, reached over to his clothes piled on the floor and grabbed a shoe. She flung it without thinking; it hit him squarely in the head and bounced to the floor. Takashi sputtered briefly, then lapsed into silence.

Even after fourteen days stuck in the dark cargo hold, subsisting on one bowl of rice gruel and a cup of water per day and forced to relieve herself in a slop bucket that was emptied only twice during the entire passage, Kikue still felt there was a way out of her predicament. She could not believe she had been sold by her parents, as Saigo said. She was convinced that they had been tricked by the unctuous Oshichi. After all, she showed her a photograph. . . .

Upon her arrival in America, Kikue was promptly delivered to Kato's office, which doubled as a storeroom in the basement of his restaurant. The low-ceilinged, windowless room was dominated by a fine oak desk the size of a bathtub, incongru-

Yoji Yamaguchi

ous amid the sacks of flour, cans of lard, and pickle jars unceremoniously stacked along the walls.

Kato was a rotund, bespectacled man in his forties who dressed more like a banker than the pimp and loan shark that he was. When he first came to these shores he had tried to fashion himself into a likeness of the American president, complete with walrus mustache and hair parted down the middle. The effect was regrettable, what with his jowly face and protruding overbite.

Kato smiled faintly, then produced a piece of paper from his top desk drawer, laid it before him and adjusted his glasses. "You work for me now," he said in a wheezy voice, perusing the paper. "I have a contract with your parents for your services. For an advance equal to three thousand dollars American (less commission and other considerations) against sixty percent of your wages (after deductions for expenses, fees, et cetera) for ten years or full repayment of the three thousand dollars—plus interest accruing at a rate of twenty-five percent annually—whichever comes first."

"Liar!" More angry than afraid, she tried to snatch the document from the desk. Kato's pudgy hand slammed down on it with surprising force. Kikue flinched, then peeked at the paper. "That's a marriage contract!"

Kato shrugged. "Ah well, I suppose you could call it that. But the terms are quite clear, and as you can see"—he flashed the contract briefly in her direction—"it has been signed and countersigned by your father and my representative, Oshichi."

Kikue pointed at the contract. "That paper means nothing.

Face of a Stranger

My father can hardly read. He couldn't have understood what he was signing."

Kato smiled wanly. "Excuse me, but he seemed to understand the payment clause well enough."

Kikue was at a loss. Was it possible? Perhaps. For as long as she could remember, her father was always complaining about the rent on their land going up and the price for their rice crop going down; and every year it seemed they had less and less to eat. But sell her? No, she thought. Other people might still sell off their daughters, but not her parents.

She thought of the Muras, an old, bilious couple who lived near her parents, and were renowned for their spectacularly loud rows that all could hear; yet they kept to themselves like hermits. The story was that they had sold their eldest daughter, their favorite, to buy their house, only to have their two remaining children, a boy and a girl, die of tuberculosis in the same year.

"What if I refuse to work for you?" she asked, throwing her head back.

Kato laughed, a harsh, deathly rattle. "You have no choice. As you are under contract to me, I'll see to it that no one here gives you a job; and you can forget about finding a husband as well. If you try to return to Japan—as if you could afford to—I'll find you—I always do. I'll let it be known wherever you are that you're a fugitive from America who murdered her husband in his sleep, stole all his money, ran off with another man, and then left him high and dry as well. A kakeochi supreme.

"Imagine your reception; no decent person would give you

Yoji Yamaguchi

the time of day. How would you live then? You'd wind up whoring anyway—only much closer to home. And you'd be amazed at the people you run into at a brothel: friends, neighbors, relatives. Think about it.

"Of course, if you can pay me back all the money I've spent to bring you over here, you won't have to work a single minute for me."

"How much is that?" Kikue asked, hoping against hope.

Kato pulled out a thick, leather-bound ledger and leisurely flipped through the pages. He stopped and adjusted his glasses. "Eeh, toh," he muttered. "Your debt to me as of now is . . . four thousand dollars American." Kikue could only stare at him as the defiance and indignation in her fled, leaving her helpless and dumb. She was about to slink out of the basement when Kato, who was replacing the ledger back in its drawer, said indifferently: "Oh, one more thing. Report to Saigo. He will assign you your new name."

She could only grunt: "Uhn?"

He looked up at her with a puzzled frown. "I said: Report-to-Saigo-for-your-new-name."

"But why do I need a new name?"

Kato sighed, closed his eyes and adjusted his glasses. His voice sounded strained. "I will be frank. Most of the girls in my service prefer to adopt new names, to protect the reputations of their families. After all, should you achieve renown for your talents—and I surely hope you will!—the word will spread quicker than the plague, and I have no doubt your parents would wish to keep their name out of it."

Kikue said nothing, and stared. Kato's voice rose in impatience. "I will be even more frank. You belong to me now. I don't want you to think of yourself as—what is it? . . . " He glanced down at the contract to find her name. ". . . as T—— anymore. That girl had a family, friends, a home. You have nobody but me, nothing but what I give you. You are nobody but who I say you are. That girl—I can't even remember her name now—no longer exists."

She was assigned the name Kikue—the second of Kato's women to be so named; her predecessor, she later learned, had died of influenza only the year before (an indication of not only Saigo's poor memory, but his decidedly bridled imagination as well).

It didn't take Kikue long to figure out that she would never be able to pay off the debt strictly according to Kato's terms. On an average month she could expect to take in between a hundred and a hundred and fifty dollars; one-third of that was automatically deducted to pay off her fare and immigration fees; one-third for her room, board, and clothes (to replace her luggage, which had mysteriously disappeared); and the rest was applied against the balance, but that amount would barely cover the interest alone. She was sure she would grow old and die paying off that debt of hers—or rather, if Kato was to be believed, of her parents.

Takashi rolled over onto his side; Kikue regarded his bare buttocks sourly. She shuddered. Quite unexpectedly, she felt all the men who had come to her in the past, crowding into her hut, inundating her with their hot stinking breath: nervous young boys flopping and twitching on top of her like fish out of water, maybe jamming her chin with a shoulder in their clumsy, frenzied haste; old men who stank of liquor and the rot of age wheezing and grunting as if they might die with their semi-erections still inside her; fat bellies pressing her like a stone; bony hips banging against her tender thighs; and—on at least two occasions—crazed hands clutching her throat, cutting off her air as she was entered from below.

Kikue leapt to her feet and inhaled sharply. She looked around the tiny room, then grabbed the slat of tin metal she used to stoke the brazier. She wrapped a rag around it for a grip, and thrust it into the coals. When the end began to glow, she lifted it from the brazier and stealthily approached the cot, drawn like a magnet to Takashi's milky white ass.

He rolled onto his back again. She stopped in her tracks; what she saw jarred her. Takashi did not look as taut and vital as when he was first brought in; he now looked flaccid, his skin pasty and jaundiced in the dim light, his limbs bony and angular, knobby at their joints. His bowleggedness was even more apparent. And Kikue pitied his poor sex, desiccated and shriveled, a miserable, puny thing.

She studied his face. It was pale, but his ears were flaming red, which made them look bigger, almost clownish. Though he was asleep, his eyelids were half-open, revealing the white undersides of his eyes. His lips were parted slightly, and Kikue noted with disgust the thin thread of drool inching out from the corner of his mouth.

And to think—this was the man whom she thought she was

23

to marry, the man she was once afraid would turn her down because she was not beautiful. Kikue wondered: what kind of husband would he have been?—running after prostitutes, drinking himself into a stupor, probably losing his job as well. She sighed; the sight of Takashi was beginning to depress her. She reached down and pulled the blanket on top of him, covering him head to toe.

A small patch of the blanket, where it covered Takashi's waist, rustled lazily, as if a small animal were burrowing underneath. Takashi was plainly scratching himself. He stopped. For some reason, she found the hidden activity funny and began tittering, then laughing aloud. She dropped the stoker to the floor.

Kikue scooped up the money on the floor. On an impulse she picked up Takashi's trousers and rummaged through the pockets. She found fifty-three dollars in all. She watched the bed intently for any sign of movement as she sidled over to the corner of the hut. Quietly, she knelt and pried up a loose floorboard; she pulled out the small box in which she stashed money whenever Kato sent his nephew Junzo around China Alley to collect his cut. She slipped the money into the box and carefully replaced it along with the plank.

She stood up and opened the door of the hut a crack. The sky was overcast, a deep purple: dawn was approaching. How long had she been sitting there, watching him sleep?

She debated whether or not to look for Saigo, have him throw Arai out into the street. Then she had an idea.

Standing over the bed, she pulled the blanket off Takashi;

then she shed her dress and tousled her hair; gingerly she lay down on top of him, as if settling down on a bed of sharp rocks. His skin was cool and clammy against hers. Takashi did not move. She blew on his forehead. No response. She pinched his nose. He twitched. She pulled on his ears. He winced. She slapped him three times across the face. His head began to nod from side to side. She lowered her face, inches above his, and shouted, "WAKE UP."

His eyes fluttered open; he blinked several times. When they registered Kikue's face hovering above his, they grew wide.

Kikue sat up and stretched. "Are you all right? I was worried," she said, slapping him playfully on the chest. "For a second I thought you died on me."

Takashi gaped at her in obvious astonishment. He lifted his head and slowly surveyed the room.

Kikue climbed off the bed, raised her arms above her head, and stretched again, groaning luxuriantly. "Neh, I've never had a man go for as long as you did," she said in her most girlish voice. She watched Takashi's face for signs of a smirk, but there were still only knitted eyebrows, a bewildered frown. She knew full well the question on his mind—*How did I get here?*—and reveled in his bafflement.

"You were wonderful."

"Oh, uh, thanks," he mumbled, and slowly sat up. The simple act made him clutch his head in pain with both hands.

She knew he would be too vain to admit his confusion. She quickly put on her dress. "I'd love to let you stay, but I have others waiting. . . ."

Face of a Stranger

He stared at her for a while, and then his eyebrows sagged in dismay as it evidently dawned on him where he was. Kikue wondered whence his chagrin: his own inability to remember anything, or just the sight of her? Calmly, she counseled herself, calmly now.

"I, uh, should go now?" he said.

"Yes, I'm sorry."

Takashi dragged his legs off the bed and lurched to his feet. Kikue gritted her teeth impatiently as she watched him dress while staggering a half-caper, first trying to put his leg through a shirtsleeve, then putting his trousers on backward three times. Twenty minutes later, when he was finally able to distinguish his left shoe from the right, her jaw was aching to the point of numbness.

His laces undone, his fly open, and his shirt buttoned crookedly, Takashi was nonetheless ready to leave. "Well, that's that, then, huh?" he said.

Kikue stood discreetly blocking the door, an expectant look on her face. "Umm. . . ." Her voice was barely audible.

"Uhn?"

"Umm. . . ."

Takashi stared at her, his eyes vacant. Kikue scowled. "Three dollars please," she finally whispered.

"Uhn?"

"Three dollars."

"Oh! But . . . I didn't pay you already?"

Kikue shook her head. "You *said* you would pay me after."

Takashi scratched his head. Unable to remember the events

Yoji Yamaguchi

of the night, he could scarcely differ with her. "Well then. . . ."
He reached into his pockets.

He frowned, perplexed. His frantic hands groped his pockets,
patted his shirt pocket and his coat, but came up empty. "Um, I
don't seem . . . I don't know . . . I lost . . . I have no money," he
declared, his voice choked with embarrassment.

Kikue marveled at his stupidity: it never once occurred to
him that he might have been ripped off. For an instant she felt
something like pity for him, and was briefly tempted to end the
subterfuge and tell him all. But she knew if she did she would
never see him again, and for reasons not wholly clear to her,
she understood that would never do.

So, she let her lip quiver before falling to her knees and bury-
ing her face in her hands. "Oh, you tricked me!" she wailed.
"You awful man, you lied to me!"

"But . . ." Takashi tried to protest.

"Now I'm undone—and so are you! Kato will beat me for not
bringing in money; and he'll have you beaten, too, for not paying for your time! Oh, what will I do?" she sobbed.

"Beaten?" He gaped at her, a stricken look on his face.

So, Kikue thought, he's a coward as well. "Yes," she hissed.
"You should have seen what they did to the last man who tried
to get away without paying. Neh, I never knew a man could
bleed so much!"

"Bleed?"

She nodded vigorously, cupping her hands over her ears. "I
can still hear him screaming. Oh, how terrible!"

Takashi's face blanched, and his mouth hung open. "Well,

Face of a Stranger

does he have to know . . . about me?" he asked finally, in a meek voice.

"Oh, he always knows! His men see everybody who comes and goes! And you were the only one here tonight!"

Takashi sat heavily on the bed. His shoulders sagged. "What will I do?"

Kikue did not fail to notice that he was concerned only with his own hide. But she was enjoying his panic too much to be angry. She stood up and took his hands. "Neh, this is what you must do," she said in a reassuring voice, pulling him to his feet. "Come back tomorrow night before midnight with the money. They won't collect before then. But you have to bring it or we'll both be dead." She let go of his hands and stepped around him, then pulled the cot away from the wall. "See that? It's a trap door, for people who don't want to be seen leaving."

Kato had added an escape door to all of the huts after that regrettable incident with Mr. Matsuda's wife, who followed him one night to China Alley and burst into the hut he was patronizing at a most unpropitious moment, catching her husband quite literally with his pants down.

"Go out through there. It'll be better if they don't see you leaving. And use it when you come back tomorrow night, too. Now go, hurry." She pushed Takashi toward the corner. Reluctantly, he dropped to his hands and knees and crawled—promptly banging his head against the unyielding door.

"It opens in," Kikue called out cheerfully. "You have to pull."

Rubbing his pate, Takashi pulled the door open and slipped

out into the night. The sight of him crawling away gave Kikue a little satisfaction.

But it was not nearly enough. She hoped he would be back. The prospect excited her; she was still not entirely certain why. But the elements of an idea—fluid, inchoate—were slowly gathering in her head.

two

Takashi was in hell. From the moment he left the boarding house where he lived and set out for the home of Joan and Jane Warren, the twin sisters who employed him, he was visited by one torment after another.

It wasn't enough that his head was pounding from a hangover; or that to his bleary eyes the ground before him seemed to recede as he walked, making him feel as if his head were on backward; or that he was pelted by a cold rain that stank to him, oddly, of rotten eggs.

When he entered through the back door of the Warren house, he was greeted by their dog, Woodrow, a black, rotund, short-legged, greasy-haired mongrel, with rheumy, blood-shot eyes, brown teeth, and putrid breath. He barked menacingly, his hackles raised and his tail down. He had not grown accustomed to Takashi yet; or else, he simply did not like him.

"Chaaarliee—is that you?" two tremulous voices trilled in unison from the next room.

On his first day as their houseboy, they dubbed him "Charlie" after "Arai" and even plain old "Takashi" proved too difficult for their thick *hakujin* tongues. He did not know that his predecessor was also renamed "Charlie," as were all the Issei houseboys who worked for the Warrens.

When they appeared in the kitchen together, Takashi could not help but blink. As difficult as it was for him to distinguish one identical twin from the other, he thought for a moment that he was seeing double: the two women were dressed exactly alike, in matching drab green dresses. He looked down at Woodrow, who was panting and drooling, lips bared in what looked like a shit-eating grin.

For breakfast, Joan (or Jane) asked for an omelette with cheese and onions, fried ham, toast with preserves; Jane (or Joan) asked for a bowl of oatmeal and berries topped with sugar. Takashi, his mind still muddy, his English inept, and his culinary skill nonexistent, confused everything. To the sisters' dismay, he gave Joan (or Jane) an omelette stuffed with berries and a slice of ham crusted with burnt black jam; while Jane (or Joan) got a slab of cheese floating in a bowl of oatmeal and a plate of onions dusted with sugar.

To be fair, Takashi was also distracted by what the prostitute had said: *I never knew a man could bleed so much. . . .*

As the morning progressed, his worry burgeoned. The threat

Yoji Yamaguchi

of Kato's reprisals chilled him to the bone. Where would he get the money? Asking his employers was out of the question; the parsimonious old hags would not give him a dime one second before the agreed-upon payday and time, which was three days, eight and a half hours away. Besides, he did not know the English words for *advance* or *loan*; they were not to be found in his copy of *Beikoku Rodo Benran*, Shimizu's English guide for houseboys.

Memories of the prostitute came to him as he worked, and he blushed in shame and vexation at his inability to remember anything of his encounter. Her voice in his mind made him wince and smart as if he were being pricked by sharp forks. *Oh, you terrible man . . . you were wonderful . . . now I am undone . . . I'd love to have you stay. . . .* He did not know what to make of her, why she troubled him so.

As if he were not suffering enough already, his bosses seemed to be doing their best to contribute to his misery. Jane (Joan?) asked for tea, while Joan (Jane?) demanded her shawl. By the time the water was boiling, he forgot who wanted which.

When he brought Jane/Joan her tea in the sitting room, she said incredulously: "What's this? I asked you to bring me my shawl. *Shawl.* Not tea."

Almost simultaneously, he heard Joan/Jane calling from upstairs: "Charlie, where's my tea? What's taking you so long?"

An hour later, one of them (he didn't care which) instructed him to sweep the front porch. No sooner had he begun when the other one (or was it?) stuck her head out the door and told him to polish the silver.

Face of a Stranger

Takashi had heard from men who worked on the plantations in Hawaii about the *luna* or *haole*—the *hakujin* foreman—who cracked whips over the heads, and occasionally on the backs, of field hands to persuade them to work faster. And yet, he thought, a whip might be preferable to the lashes he had to endure every day: "Chaar-lie . . . this is . . . overcooked"; "Chaar-lie . . . you missed . . . a spot"; "Hur-ry, Chaar-lie . . . you are working . . . too slow"—always uttered with the tortuous slowness and painstaking precision most people use to communicate with idiots and little children.

As he was polishing a mirror, he stopped to examine himself in his domestic's uniform—white shirt and pants a size too small, with matching gloves and a black bow tie. Oh, if his old nanny Aya could see the young *danna* washing windows, polishing silverware, serving tea and biscuits on a lace-covered settee or scooping up after Woodrow in plain view of the neighbors—what a laugh she would have at his expense!

To be wanting at an arduous job is an embarrassment; to be inadequate at a job wholly unworthy of one's toil is total humiliation. His strong, sinewy hands were not made for darning socks or scrubbing pots; his sturdy, rock-hard back was not designed for stooping over a wash basin, nor were his perfect knees meant to scrape across a kitchen floor. Exactly what his purpose was, Takashi didn't know, but he was certain he was born for something better than this.

The day grew worse and worse. His first task after lunch was to spread fresh manure in the backyard garden, even though rain was still falling steadily. Cursing to the winds, he pushed a

Yoji Yamaguchi

wheelbarrow heaped with manure so fresh it was practically steaming. The garden itself was like a fen. As soon as he began shoveling shit onto the ground, he found himself sinking in the ooze, up to the tops of his ankles. Each step he took was a contest with the ground, which sucked tenaciously at his feet. Manure and mud began to mix, an unholy stew.

Unexpectedly, he remembered the first prostitute, the young one who accosted him in the alley and called him "husband"; he heard the other man laughing, taunting *ain't you got a job of your own?* Takashi looked down at himself, soaked and muddy, knee-deep in muck. He felt a pang in his stomach, palpable as a jabbing hook.

He thought of the other prostitute again. She was older than him, though not as old as the ghoul Wada. She was not beautiful. And yet she was kind. *Neh, this is what you must do. . . .* In spite of his misery, he felt a rustling in his pants. Desperately, he tried to remember her in bed.

"Chaarliee," the querulous voice called from the house. Takashi dropped his shovel and struggled to extricate himself from the mire.

He stopped at the back door and bowed. "Hai," he said in his most subservient voice.

The old woman did not seem to notice his wretched appearance. "Charlie, now . . . go to . . . the farmers' market . . . and buy . . . vegetables. Here . . . is the list." She held out a piece of paper gingerly with her fingers, as if offering a scrap to a wild dog. Her nose wrinkled slightly, no doubt at the odor of his soiled clothes.

Takashi took the list and bowed again. "Ah aan-da-staan," he drawled, as slowly and idiotically as she had.

Just then the other sister appeared at the door. "Jane, what's this? I wanted Charlie to fertilize the garden."

"Well, we need vegetables for dinner."

"But the garden . . . "

"Oh, Joan, don't be silly. He's wasting his time. The rain is just washing the fertilizer away."

As he watched and listened to the two *hakujin* women argue, mirror images of one another, Takashi briefly felt as if he were going insane.

By the time Takashi reached the farmers' market the rain had stopped, and a cold wind from the northeast blew away most of the cloud cover. But it was too late for the farmers' good; the crowd remained sparse, only a handful of customers picking listlessly through the bushels of produce on display. No one noticed the pathetic figure Takashi cut, shivering in his soggy, muddy houseboy's uniform.

He was poking at a stack of cabbages in the bed of a farmer's truck under the glare of its owner when he heard a low rumbling voice: "Arai-san! Arai-san!"

It was Kogoro Doi. Kogoro leased a three-acre tract of dry, silty land next to the coastal road. The fourth and youngest son of a poor fisherman from an obscure village in the north of Japan, Kogoro was regarded by the other local Issei with a mixture of scorn and fear: scorn, because he was a bumpkin, slow-witted, gullible to a fault; fear, because at six foot three and 250

36

pounds he towered over his compatriots like a giant. He was dressed that day in overalls, a flannel coat, and a floppy-brimmed straw hat that one would normally find on a scarecrow.

As he approached Kogoro's truck, Takashi was seized with a fit of shivering. Soaked to the bone, he noticed for the first time how cold he was. He hunched his shoulders and dug his hands into his pockets.

"Hello, hello," Kogoro brayed. "Got some nice lettuce today." He held up two heads of lettuce that were as large as a grown man's skull. In his truck were also bushels full of oversize tomatoes and cabbages that dwarfed those of his neighbors. Kogoro's crops were a source of wonder and envy among the local farmers; it seemed as if everything he planted mimicked its caretaker, growing to freakish proportions.

Takashi opened his mouth to reply, but his teeth began to chatter uncontrollably. "Ah . . . ah . . . ah" was all he could stammer. A wave of dizziness swept over him; his legs felt weak, his head empty.

Kogoro stared at him quizzically. "Uhn?"

"Ah . . . ah . . . ah. . . ."

"You don't look so good," Kogoro mumbled.

Takashi glared and tried to retort, but his jaw would not obey him. "Ah . . . ah . . . ah. . . ."

Kogoro peered at him. "You're all wet," he declared.

Takashi rolled his eyes and clamped his mouth shut.

"Aren't you cold?"

As if in reply, Takashi let fly an explosive sneeze, spraying the farmer squarely in the face.

Face of a Stranger

But Kogoro was unfazed. Without a word, he dropped his prize lettuce, shed his coat, and wrapped it around Takashi's shoulders, taking him by surprise. The huge coat engulfed him; to his revulsion, the cloth reeked of—what else?—fertilizer.

When Takashi tried to shuck the garment, Kogoro clapped his massive hands on his shoulders; Takashi's knees nearly buckled from the unintended force of the blows.

"Iya, iya," Kogoro protested. "You keep it on. I don't need it."

Takashi felt ready to gag. He could feel the smell of manure permeating his skin, right down to the bone, from his frozen, mud-caked feet up to his burning nostrils. Wrapped thus in ordure, he could almost feel himself decomposing as well.

Then, in the midst of that hell, he found something like salvation. It was there, in Kogoro's worried expression, the arc of his thick brows and the sagging corners of his mouth; and in the firm grip with which he held the coat around Takashi's shoulders. Takashi could see that Kogoro was the type who would give his shirt to someone who had just robbed him of his trousers.

Even in his worst misery, Takashi had not forgotten for a moment the problem of Kato and the money. The old women had given him money to buy produce, but embezzling a single cent of it never once occurred to him: such is the trepidation of a slave. Instead, he had another idea.

Takashi's head sagged, and he covered his face with both hands. His shoulders heaved, and he let out a short sob. He peeked out of the corner of his eye, between his fingers, at Kogoro: the farmer looked puzzled. Takashi sobbed again, louder. Still the same imbecilic look! Takashi could not stand it. He cut loose a long, undulating wail.

Kogoro gaped in dismay. "Something wrong?" he asked.

"Oh, I am ashamed!" Takashi howled. "I've disgraced myself, my family, my country! I can never be forgiven!"

"Uhn?"

"I am worthless; I am not fit to live!"

"I don't understand."

"I was entrusted by my bosses, the Ladies Warren, with money to buy vegetables. A simple errand, neh? But"—he choked back a sob—"now the money is lost and I . . . I am to blame! I failed them!"

"But . . . I don't understand."

"On my way here I was waylaid by three men. They beat me and robbed me of my coat and the money my bosses gave me. Then they threw me into a ditch. Look." Takashi sniffed and tugged at his muddy pants. "I was too weak to protect my bosses' property. Too weak to defend my honor."

"Uh, well, shikata ga nai. Can't be helped, I guess."

"But I should have been able to fend off four men."

"Oh, but I thought you said . . . "

"How can I face the Ladies Warren without the produce I was supposed to buy, or the money? How can I explain that the money is lost and I am still alive, that I did not give my life doing my duty, fighting off that gang of five?"

"You mean four . . . "

"My shame is unendurable. What will I do?" Takashi fell to his knees and began to weep.

He expected it would take the farmer at least three minutes to figure out what he should do. To Takashi's mild surprise, it took Kogoro all of thirty seconds before he uttered the words Takashi was so anxious to hear: "How much did they take from you?"

So moved was Kogoro by Takashi's distress that he gave him six dollars instead of the three dollars he had asked for—every cent that he had on him at the moment—and a bushel of vegetables gratis, over Takashi's not-too-vehement protests.

As he walked back to the Warren house with his haul, Takashi felt as elated as he had after winning at *fan-tan*. He was excited at the prospect of returning to China Alley, now that he had enough money not only to pay for the night before, but that night as well. He assumed that his dizziness and the feverish heat coursing through his blood were merely the giddy symptoms of triumph and lust.

Kikue lay exhausted on the soft down mattress as sunlight filtered in through the lace window curtains. She stretched languorously and sighed. On the nightstand beside the bed sat a tray stacked with empty dishes, the remnants of a copious breakfast of ham steak, eggs, rolls, and strawberries.

She rolled over, curled up in a fetal position, rubbing her cheek against the clean cotton pillowcase. Breakfast had been superb, as it always was at the Pacific Hotel, the small, thirteen-room boardinghouse run by the Inada family where she resided.

Kikue's living arrangement was, to say the least, unusual. All the other prostitutes lived in the shacks from which they worked. The Pacific Hotel, on the other hand, catered to Issei bachelors of impeccable reputation, preferably Christian. Scurrilous rumors floated around town that the Inadas demanded letters of reference from a minister and a deacon (Buddhist recommendations were occasionally accepted), and that one had to bow and chant the names of the Father, Son, and Holy Ghost three times before checking in. But it was a fact that gamblers, drunks, and persons of ill-repute were not welcome at the Pacific Hotel.

So how did it come to pass that a prostitute was living in the top-floor suite—twice as big as any of the other rooms, fully accoutred with a walk-in closet and a fake Persian rug—in this righteous family's inn?

Much to Kikue's and the other women's good fortune, Kato charged his nephew Junzo with the task of collecting his cut from the prostitutes' wages. Junzo was a sickly youth who nearly died from a bout of pneumonia in infancy. Those who knew him wondered to what extent this early trauma affected his brain, for in addition to being pale, skinny, and perpetually ill, he was also prodigiously dim. So hapless was he that his father could not even buy the boy's way into the lowliest gang.

His mother, Kato's imperious eldest sister, took it upon herself to secure her son's future. She fairly dumped poor Junzo on his uncle's doorstep along with a sternly worded letter to her brother requesting he find suitable employment for her son—no small task, given Junzo's limited ken.

What does a gangster do with a slug of a relative on his hands? His business was no place for the faint of heart or the

Face of a Stranger

slow of wit. If something happened to Junzo, Kato knew that his sister would make him pay dearly. He finally decided to let his no-account nephew oversee the hookers, figuring that, if nothing else, he could at least handle a woman.

It was a miscalculation: Junzo was no match for women who had learned by experience to spot easy marks as keenly as sharks sniff out blood. They called him *Momotaro*, Peach Boy, among other insults, and used him unabashedly. At the end of each week, when he came by to collect, they hiked up their skirts and occasionally flashed their breasts, laughing as the sweat burst from his crimson face and he stammered and shoved his quaking hands into his pockets, fumbling to conceal his tumescence. Because Kato took his cut by charging a percentage rather than a flat fee, they were able to skim from him liberally; poor Junzo, who could scarcely count, was none the wiser. Whenever he tried to take a hard line, dropping his squeaky voice down an octave or two, they sometimes wept fecund tears that quickly eroded his resolve, but more often they simply routed him from their rooms with a fusillade of insults and mockery.

Whenever pressed by his uncle to explain his meager take, Junzo, embarrassed by his powerlessness over the women, would only mumble that business was slow. Kato knew better; he could not begin to calculate how much the boy was costing him each month. But there was nothing to be done. Rightly fearing his sister's wrath, he did not dare show up Junzo's incompetence in front of the whores, or even so much as reprimand him and risk injuring his delicate feelings.

Kato was briefly tempted to send in his muscle, Saigo, to

teach these impudent women a thing or two about respect but decided against it. It would have made no sense for him to put his own work force out of commission, after all; that would have left the door open for one of his rivals to swoop in with his own covey and take over his turf. Besides, the *hakujin* would not have taken kindly to such a pogrom; he knew well enough that in America a *Nihonjin*—especially a crooked one—had to be as inconspicuous as possible if he wanted to get ahead.

Thus Kikue and the others could get away with paying as little as one-fifth of what Kato claimed as his due. Part of this modest windfall she wired each month to her parents through the local Keihin Bank. But she could not bring herself to write to them yet.

She had assumed Kato had duped her and her parents; hadn't the old woman Oshichi shown her Takashi's picture and said, "This is your husband-to-be"? After a week of servicing the priapic needs of the Japanese immigrants, however, she wasn't so sure. Her doubts were pounded home daily by the indignities visited upon her, and she could neither eat nor sleep. But habit dulls even the most keenly whetted outrage, especially in the absence of succor and rest. After two months or so in America, for a time Kikue forgot her parents altogether, became in fact the nonperson Kato was seeking.

Then she began to notice her colleagues making their weekly pilgrimages to wire money home to their families. This phenomenon vexed her almost as much as the question of her parents' culpability, for unlike her, most of these women had been brazenly purchased, without pretenses. She could not understand why they still felt obliged to give over nearly all of their meager earnings to their families, who had sold them off in the first place.

Finally she approached one of them, a young, somewhat plump woman with the regrettable name of Hako (Saigo's idea of a bawdy joke).

"Why not?" Hako replied, when asked why she wired money home. "What am I going to do with it—take a boat to Brazil?" She laughed.

"But why give it to your parents? They got you into this mess, after all."

Hako shrugged. "When you're starving you'll do anything to anyone. At least they didn't drown me in a pond."

"Maybe it would have been just as well—for all of us."

Hako scowled. "Why are you so proud?" Startled by her anger, Kikue had no reply.

Hako went on: "Look, I'm not doing it to be a nice girl. Didn't Fat Pig give you his speech about forgetting who you are? Well, I send money home so I don't forget. I tell myself 'I'm supporting my family' and it lets me think that I'm something else besides the senpu working out of a hut." A contemplative look crossed her face, making her look years older in an instant, until her round face crinkled into a smile. "And besides, no matter what my parents did, at least they gave me a proper name—they didn't call me 'Pussy.'" She burst out laughing, and Kikue could not help but join her. Briefly, she was tempted to ask Hako what that proper name might be, but decided it would be nosy.

So Kikue began sending her parents a cut each month, albeit anonymously, without any letter. What would she write, after all? "I entertained forty-two men this week. My back is aching, but the money is great." No, it would not do. She would support them, yes, but she had nothing to tell them. They became abstractions to her, like dead spirits almost, alive but not alive, and each month when she went to the bank to wire them money, she felt almost as if she were casting a lantern onto the waters.

Kikue began to accumulate money. Unlike the others, who spent their meager windfalls on trifles such as stockings, perfumes, and combs, she intended to use her money to pay off Kato once and for all and then leave him—to do what, she didn't know; she would figure that out later. But after three years, during which time she had saved barely four hundred dollars, she realized it wasn't enough simply to bilk Junzo of pocket change every week. She needed to make her money beget more money.

Banks were out of the question, since the managers of both Japanese-owned banks in town were regulars at China Alley and (it was rumored) Kato's silent partners; they would have surely informed him if a supposedly penniless prostitute were to open a large account at one of their banks. A *tanomoshi* would not do, either; these credit associations were close-knit affairs, usually among people from the same hometown or home prefecture, and would hardly be likely to admit a prostitute.

Then she was visited one night by a distraught young man so distracted by his woes that he could not perform and began to

Face of a Stranger

cry shamefully. Perhaps because she did not laugh, or throw him out into the night, or maybe simply because she asked "What's wrong?" he blurted out to her his awful secret.

It seems that before coming to America he had been engaged to be married. Both families agreed that he would emigrate to America, then send for his bride after five years, the length of time they all estimated it would take him to establish himself in a well-paying job and buy a nice home. The five years went by and he found himself still working as a field hand, living in a bunkhouse. He would have liked to put off his marriage a few years, until his situation was more certain, but his betrothed would have none of it. She had waited long enough, she wrote to him, and she was not getting any younger; in fact, already her cousins were starting to call her Old Maid (she was twenty-one at the time). His financial straits did not discourage her in the least; in fact, they only made her more anxious to come over. "It's because you're a bachelor that you've been so lazy," she averred. No, her word was final: they had an agreement and she expected him to live up to it.

Alas, the young man sobbed, he couldn't. Thanks to a new agreement between the United States and Japan to curb the influx of "undesirables," it was tougher than ever to bring one's bride to America. A man had to show that his liquid assets were no less than eight hundred dollars American to secure a visa for his wife. Kikue's disconsolate caller needed three hundred dollars right away, to have enough "show money" to satisfy the authorities—and, more important, his bride-to-be.

As Kikue listened to his pitiful tale, it occurred to her that

Yoji Yamaguchi

she could lend money at interest. A few years earlier, the idea would have been unthinkable; as a child, she learned from her father's incessant tirades that moneylenders were vermin, vipers, parasites, the scum of the earth. But she was no longer that man's daughter; she was now Kikue, a prostitute living in America, and there was nothing she would not, or could not, do.

When Kikue had murmured "Maybe I can help you," the young man started, then jerked around to survey the squalid little room like a man coming out of a dream. He gawked at Kikue, then whispered: "What?"

"I said maybe I can help you."

He leaned back, cocked his head and scowled, one eyebrow arched, lips tightly pursed. Kikue could hardly chide him for his arrogance; after all, who ever heard of a whore offering alms to her john? Instead, she stepped to the corner of the room, pulled up a loose plank from the floor, and extracted an old cigar box. From this she produced a thick wad of bills.

The young man's eyes widened. "Where did you get that?" he demanded bluntly.

Kikue said: "Oh, one of my regular guests, he's a rich businessman just come over. He's so generous—not like you buranke katsugi types." She couldn't resist the dig.

The young man scarcely noticed; he was still transfixed so intently by the proffered money that she feared he might take it from her by force. She started talking fast. "I'll let you borrow what you need for six months, enough time to bring your bride over; you can start paying it back by the month or pay it back all at once in six months; either way, I don't care, so long as I get it all back—plus ten percent interest. You don't have to put anything down in advance. What do you say?"

He blinked, then said, in a surprisingly even voice: "Why would you do this for me?"

To make money off you, of course, Kikue thought. But why, she didn't fully know. He meant nothing to her; she didn't even know his name. Nor did she feel a whit of pity for him: after all, he came to her for a quick lay at a good price and nothing more. She couldn't even be sure he wasn't running a con game of his own. All reason was against it, but Kikue decided to lend him the money anyway. She had nothing to lose, after all; what good was her money when she needed ten times that? She replied: "Maybe someday you'll do a favor for me."

He accepted her offer, finally, and only then did he introduce himself. "My name is Inada Masajiro," he said formally, adding a slight, almost polite, bow.

They drew up a contract on cheap stationery Kikue had bought for the letter to her parents she never wrote. Inada pledged to repay the loan in full, plus interest, in the next six months, with an added charge of two percent a month for any unpaid balance after the loan came due. When the deal was consummated, he took his money and backed out of the shack, flustered and dumb, bowing excessively. Only after he was gone did Kikue realize that he had not paid for his visit.

After six months went by and he (and her money) failed to materialize, Kikue berated herself mercilessly: *Duped yet again.* At first she suspected that he was one of Kato's men, sent to steal back what she had stolen, but somehow it didn't wash

The chubby, round-faced fellow did not look like a typical Kato man (Junzo notwithstanding), and his tears were not the tears of a con man. Or so she thought.

Another explanation occurred to her: the man was in the business himself, and used her money to lure some other woman to America. It was horrible for her to contemplate.

Almost a year to the day of his original visit, the young man showed up at her shack. He bowed and gathered himself. "Please forgive me: I have been terribly negligent in the matter of my debt to you. You see, shortly after my wife arrived in America, we were presented with a wonderful opportunity—to own a hotel here in town. My father was an innkeeper back in Japan, and it has always been a wish of mine to follow his footsteps.

"In order to realize this dream, though, we had to place a sizable down payment. I took the liberty of using the money you had so generously lent me. It was wrong of me to take advantage of your kindness that way—but, well, few people would have been so ready to help a stranger like you were. I hoped that you would understand if I imposed on you for just a little while longer." He paused.

Ah, now I get my money back, Kikue thought, relieved. She wondered if he remembered the two percent penalty.

But she was soon disappointed. Inada went on: "The hotel is now beginning to show signs of flourishing, but in addition to your loan, we had to take out a large mortgage. Our payments are quite severe, and money remains scarce, I'm afraid. Still, I would like to repay your kindness as best I can.

49

"I am a member of the Japanese Methodist Church. Our church runs a mission for, ah, misguided women such as yourself, and we would be most gratified if you were to give up this shack and take sanctuary there. You would be clothed and fed, you could take instruction in English—as well as the Gospel, of course—and our congregation would help you find legitimate work. You can stay there until you are able to afford to live in a decent place of your own, among Japanese of good standing. It is a tremendous opportunity, really."

Christians! Kikue vaguely knew about them and their crusade against Kato and his men, petitioning the consulate and the Americans to deport him, demonstrating in the streets, forcing him to spend a fortune each year on bail money for his underlings. No one knew for sure, but nearly everyone agreed that it was Kato's men who recently smashed the windows and left a dung pile on the doorstep of one of the churches.

Kikue imagined herself at one of the temperance rallies these Christians were so fond of holding, wearing a brown potato sack of a dress and maybe a big floppy hat as well, pounding on a tambourine and singing one of their songs in English. She almost burst out laughing.

Inada went on: "At first, I had no qualms about using your money for the down payment, even though our deal was that I would repay you as soon as I was safely married. It took me a while, but I figured out that the story about your 'client' was, ah, perhaps an exaggeration, and your claim to the money was not, eh, all that valid. Thus, you were not in a position to demand satisfaction. And since you didn't look like you were going to do anything with it, I thought it meet that I make something good out of what was clearly bad.

"But you must believe me when I say I fully intend to repay you once the hotel begins to show a reasonable profit. Right now we are just breaking even."

Kikue was puzzled. "So why did you come back at all? Why not just make a clean getaway? And why put me up in your church?"

Inada seemed to bristle at her first two questions. "I am indebted to you, not just for the money; after all, without you I would not have my hotel. You were willing to help though you didn't have to. Now I believe I can help you."

Kikue looked at him askance.

"There is more," he said. "You see, ah, when we first met, I had not yet learned the Way of the Lord. It was my wife who taught me, opened my eyes. She is, uh, a woman of the strictest morals, you see, and—"

"She doesn't know about me," Kikue said, cutting him off.

Inada flinched in surprise, then looked down at his shoes. "So. Were she to find out that I used your money to acquire the hotel, and that I visited you in the first place for . . ." His voice trailed off in embarrassed silence.

At once Kikue understood: he was afraid she would blackmail him. The idea would have been funny were he not reneging on his debt. His offer of salvation appealed to her not at all: she would free herself from Kato on her own, of this she was determined. For the moment, though, she wanted something of equal value for her money.

Then it occurred to her. "I don't want to go to any convent," she said. "But maybe you can get me out of this shack."

Inada frowned. "I don't understand."

"I need a place to live." She smiled a smile to break men's hearts.

Inada's face sagged. "You're not serious."

"Why not? It is partly my hotel, after all."

"But . . . what would I tell my wife, my guests?"

"I'm sure you'll think of something. Tell them you're trying to make me a Christian."

Inada was beside himself, but he had little choice. As long as he was in her debt, and fearful of having his secret loan revealed to his wife, he could not deny her. So Kikue moved into his hotel's biggest room on the top floor, while he and his family lived in the basement—an arrangement that did little to assuage Mrs. Inada's suspicion or resentment toward her. And because it was left to stupid Junzo to monitor the comings and goings of the women on China Alley, Kato was none the wiser.

She wasn't sure if Inada had anything to do with it, but soon she began to receive callers who came solely to tell their financial woes to her; they would not even get around to taking their pants off. She learned how Mr. M. needed to repair the icebox in his butcher shop; how Mr. Y. was looking to buy a new tractor for his farm; how Mr. N. wanted to lease the store adjacent to his tailor shop. Soon she had a string of borrowers, all of them like Inada—family men, churchgoers, members in good standing of the Japanese Merchants' Association. Her latest customer was a surprise: Kogoro Doi, the hick from the country, who borrowed four hundred dollars to buy a truck.

She had other men approach her, too, unsavory types like Messrs. F., S., and G., with their heavy gambling and drinking debts; to them she offered condolences, maybe a quick thrill for their money, and nothing more. She decided right away that she would only lend to men who had reason to fear her, reason enough to pay back every cent and keep their mouths shut. A man in deep with the *gorotsuki*, about to get his legs broke—or worse—wouldn't be overly concerned about repaying a prostitute working on her own, she reasoned.

A soft knock on the door aroused Kikue from her torpor. It was Inada, come to collect the dishes. Kikue smiled, as she always did whenever he had to wait on her. Then she thought of Arai, and covered her mouth to keep from laughing aloud.

three

Shino was an inveterate teller of tales. Often Kikue would steal over to her hut, and they would lower the blind to keep away intruders, dim the lamp, and huddle around the smouldering brazier. It was hard for Kikue not to spend whole evenings listening to her.

Only seventeen, Shino had been in America almost as long as Kikue yet still possessed the youthful looks, the irrepressible nature, the sharp tongue and guile she had brought with her when she was thirteen. Perhaps more important, she also had the uncanny knack of discovering Kato's secrets, and it was thanks to her that the women of China Alley were invariably one step ahead of their boss. Whenever Kato planned to hike his levies on the women, business would mysteriously suffer and their earnings drop precipitously, and he would wind up taking in scarcely more, and sometimes less, than before. When Junzo made one of his surprise visits, he usually found the women ready and waiting for him, much to his bewilderment.

"Guess who I saw last night," Shino said excitedly as soon as Kikue had taken a seat on the floor.

Kikue studied her for a moment, then replied: "I'd say you saw your would-be husband."

Shino gawked. "How did you know?" Kikue merely shrugged.

Shino thrust out her lower lip; her eyes narrowed. "Neh, when did you become a seer?" she muttered.

Kikue giggled at Shino's disappointment. "I saw him, too."

"You saw him? When? Where? Did you say anything to him?" the younger woman asked breathlessly.

"Last night. He was in my hut. He talked . . . a little. His name is Arai, by the way. Arai Takashi."

Shino frowned. "He was in your hut? What was he doing there?"

Kikue laughed. "What do you think?"

Shino's body sagged, and she glowered darkly at the embers. Kikue at first assumed that Shino was angry at her for entertaining the man whose face had caused them so much pain and regret. But after recounting her confrontation with Arai, Shino blurted out, in a voice mixed with tones of jealousy and astonishment, "He ran away from me and went to see you?"

"Not exactly," Kikue said. She in turn told Shino about the three mischievous drunks who brought Arai to her.

Shino's expression softened. She smiled, then tittered, then laughed out loud at Kikue's account. When Kikue described him crawling out the trap door, Shino clapped her hands in childish delight.

"Bravo!" she cried. "What will you do if he comes back—cut his balls off? Shove a hot poker up his ass?"

Kikue shuddered. "How awful!"

Shino peered at her. "But you have to do something. It isn't enough that you took his money. He has to pay more than that. I mean . . . you can't just . . . aren't you even going to tell him that we're on to him?"

"Of course—but at the right time. But we can't get carried away: that won't do. Better to cut off Kato's balls, or Saigo's, than his, after all. He was probably as much of a dupe as any of us."

"Don't be so sure," Shino murmured.

"Neh, he probably sold his picture without knowing what for."

Shino scowled. "Why are you defending him?"

"I'm not, I just—"

"Maybe you're really in love with him?"

"Oh, don't be stupid. . . ."

"Neh, as good as he looks in the picture, he looks twice as good in the flesh. And you got to see everything. Pretty exciting!"

"Enough! I'll decide what to do about Arai later. Not now. I don't want to think about him right now. Tell me some news instead."

Shino lowered her voice down to a dramatic whisper: "I hear

Face of a Stranger

talk that the old bitch Oshichi bagged herself another pigeon. A real beauty, young, only seventeen or so, and she really knows how to turn on the charm. Oshichi was practically drooling over her.

"Trouble is, this prize bird turned out to be all crow. She was fine when they packed her up and shipped her off. But when the boat landed, the Americans boarded the ship and found the girl because she was screaming and yelling at the hakujin sailors. So they kept her at Angel Island. But you know the Americans. They might have let her pass if she hadn't started demanding a private room when they brought her to the barracks. Can you believe that: a private room on Angel Island! She made such a stink about bunking with eighty women and kids in one little room and having no privacy at all that they finally obliged her."

"Really?"

"Uhn—they stuck her in a locked closet. They're keeping her in there until they get around to deporting her. Kato is beside himself about the whole thing—he doesn't want to lose his investment, but he doesn't want a mad dog on his hands, either. He's already fired Oshichi over this mess. Serves the old bitch right, I say.

"Anyway, I hear the Americans are having trouble convincing the government to take the girl back; the consulate is saying she's really a stowaway from Hong Kong, or something like that. I guess they think she's making the whole country look bad."

"Ehh . . . does anybody know who she is?" Kikue asked.

"She's a rich girl—I hear her father's a department head at a big cotton mill. They say she was always a little wild. Acted more like a boy than a girl, supposedly. I hear she ran away from home. But beautiful, they say—the likes of which you've never seen." Shino stopped and leaned back, signifying an end.

"So, what's Kato doing about it?" Kikue asked.

"Nothing—he can't do anything," Shino replied.

"Why not?"

"Because he's been greasing palms here and back in Japan for years; that's how come none of us ever had a problem getting in," Shino explained. "Seems one of his contacts in the consulate told him to walk away from this one, 'cause she was already making too big a stink for everybody."

"So he's just going to forget about her—all that money?"

Shino shrugged. "He's been losing money on us for the past few years, thanks to the little shithead. And now that the Americans are starting to crack down, it's getting so that we just aren't worth it.

"Truth is, Kato's flat broke, and now his friends at the banks are turning their backs on him; even the loan sharks in San Francisco won't talk to him. I think he's starting to lose his mind. First he imported a thousand barrels of sake to sell over here; cost him a bundle to find out that the Americans won't touch the stuff. Then he dumped another pile of money on some silk farm in Alaska; that turned out to be nothing but a scam, of course. All he has is what he makes off the gamblers and us, and that's barely enough to meet his payroll. And if he couldn't pay Saigo, he'd leave Kato quicker than a heartbeat, and that's bad news for the old man. Without Saigo and his men, Kato's nothing."

Kikue was only half-listening. Myriad thoughts and images were running through her mind: how Arai fled when Shino called him husband—*what kind of husband are you?*; the woman on Angel Island—rich, young, beautiful, *the likes of which you've never seen;* the drunken field hand complaining about Arai—*he fancies himself irresistible to all women.* Then, the idea came to her, full-fledged, perfect.

She scarcely heard Shino talking: "Hey, are you listening to me?"

"Uhn?" Kikue blurted out, startled.

Shino frowned, indignant and not a little hurt: storyteller that she was, she expected nothing less than rapt attention from her friend.

But Kikue scarcely noticed her ire; her mind was racing now. "Was there a picture of her?"

"Uhn?" Shino was taken aback by the question and the urgency in Kikue's voice. "Who?"

"The one on the island. Is there a picture?"

"Um . . . yeah, I guess. Oshichi tried to charge Kato double her usual fee for finding her. So he wanted proof that the girl was at least half as beautiful as Oshichi had promised. She must have sent one, if her fee depended on it. Why?"

"Do you think you'd be able to get your hands on it?"

Shino leaned back and tilted her head. "What is this? What are you thinking of?"

Kikue said: "Now I know how we'll pay back Arai. I need your help."

• • •

The sanguine full moon hung low and huge. Takashi knelt in the weeds behind Kikue's hut, shivering and sweating profusely at the same time. His head felt as if it were on fire; his limbs ached as if he had been hauling rocks all day; he felt as if a rope had been cinched tightly around his chest. Takashi thought for a moment that he could hear voices inside, but decided his imagination (or his fever) was getting the better of him. He plunged forward.

As soon as he crawled through the door the crude, wooden cot flew up and away from him. In the dim lamplight of the hut he saw for not quite a second the dark form of a giant looming over him. Takashi felt himself being hoisted up by his belt into the air. The seam of his trousers felt like a cleaver embedded in his crotch, and his stomach heaved upward, pressed against his lungs. His head careened in wild gyrations.

In the first panicked instant, Takashi assumed he was being ambushed by one of Kato's men; but when he reached around to pry off the hand gripping his belt, he could feel hair on the huge knuckles, and in his delirium imagined himself in the clutches of an *oni*, the monster from his childhood nightmares. Breathless and unable to speak, he moaned in terror.

Takashi felt his body descend; when his feet touched the wooden planks of the floor, his legs buckled, and he collapsed in a heap. He heard the *oni* speak: "Arai-san?" When he looked up, he found himself staring at the wide, flat face of Kogoro Doi.

Takashi was astonished. Finding Kogoro here, in Kikue's hut, was like finding a beached whale in a tea garden. He blinked,

Face of a Stranger

feeling suspended, unreal, as if in a dream. He stood up unsteadily and regarded the farmer with unease. Kogoro began to blush furiously, and his hooded eyes fixed on his boots. Takashi glanced at the cot he was holding in one hand, as easily as a man holds his hat; Kogoro looked up and noticed Takashi and dropped the cot to the floor with a clatter, jerking his hand away as if he had been holding a snake or hot iron unawares.

Takashi felt as if he had been gulled somehow, though he was not sure why. The woman meant nothing to him; he didn't even know her name. The obvious fact that he was not her first visitor, and certainly not her last, affected him more than he cared to admit—particularly since it was Kogoro Doi, of all people. For some reason, Takashi felt Kogoro had no business there, even though he knew full well that any man with money in his pocket and a yearning in his loins did indeed have business there.

"What are you doing here?" he asked.

Kogoro froze, a panicked look on his face. Before he could respond, though, the woman started laughing. "What do you think? Kogoro's a man just like you," she said, her voice laced with mockery.

Takashi stared at the hulking farmer, who was gawking at the woman, stupefied. Man? No, not a man, a boy-giant, an overgrown child. Like me? Takashi thought. That bubble-eyed, beetle-browed, pumpkin-headed misbegotten likeness of a man? It was almost more than he could stand. He imagined Kogoro's massive bulk engulfing her lithe body and shuddered.

62

Her sweet words of the night before all but forgotten, Takashi felt like a bothersome intruder. Standing side by side, Kogoro and the tiny woman did not look as incongruous as before; instead, now he felt like the oddball, the misplaced one, who had stumbled in on two lovers. As if by magic, he began to feel as clumsy, as sluggish, and—worst of all—as ugly as Kogoro looked. He stared at the grotesque giant before him and, to his panic, could not visualize his own face.

Then Kogoro let fly a thunderous yawn. "Oh, sorry." He extracted a pocket watch from his coat and held it up to his eyes. "Ah, osokunatta, ne. I guess I should be going." Kogoro fumbled with the timepiece, an expensive gold one from the looks of it, and, forgetting where it belonged, stuffed it in his back pocket. "Kikue-san, many thanks for your, uh, hospitality. Good night," he mumbled, bowing and backpedaling to the door. Takashi winced, as much at the throbbing in his head as at Kogoro's use of the woman's name, which Takashi was learning for the first time. Kikue. And she had called him Kogoro. Takashi wondered: should I introduce myself?

The big man gingerly pushed the door open (nearly ripping it off its hinges), stumbled over the threshold and into the dark. The door slammed shut behind him, shaking the hut to its very foundations.

Takashi stared sourly at the door, then glanced over at the upended cot lying on the floor. "Look, the shithead didn't even put the bed back."

Kikue dipped her head slightly. "Onegai shimasu," she said demurely.

Face of a Stranger

Takashi grumbled as he righted the cot, which felt as heavy as a pillar of stone. Then he clumsily arranged the blankets and the straw-filled sack that served as her pillow, staggering, struggling to keep his balance. He was exhausted; the simple task of making a bed was as onerous to him as rolling a boulder up a hill.

He turned to Kikue, reached into his pocket, and handed her the money. She hesitated before taking it, then slowly leafed through the bills. Her head tilted, her eyebrows arched quizzically. "You gave me too much; it was only three dollars," she said.

"Three dollars for last night," Takashi said.

"So."

"And three for tonight."

Kikue looked up at him sharply and stumbled one step back; her eyes widened, and her jaw looked ready to fall open. Takashi was taken aback. He had assumed she would be pleased at his offer, if for no other reason than the extra money. But the look on her face—as if he had just asked her to dine on maggots—he did not expect at all. What had happened to him since the previous night, when he was *wonderful*? What had made him suddenly so repulsive that even whores wanted nothing to do with him—not even for money?

"Is something wrong?" he asked peevishly.

"Er . . . no . . . not at all . . . please . . . " she stammered as she beckoned him to the bed, feebly waving her hand as if shooing a fly.

A wave of dizziness and nausea rushed through Takashi. His

Yoji Yamaguchi

trembling body was soaked with sweat. He felt as if someone had put a hex on him, robbing him not only of his strength, but also of his very body. He collapsed onto the bed. The hard, unyielding mattress, such as it was, felt unusually warm and comfortable. He wanted to sleep. He forgot about Kikue, the money, Kogoro.

Instead, he heard his mother telling him in her flat, monotone voice to quit their home. "If you want to go to America, that's fine; but it will be some time before you can think of coming back, I'm afraid. Your father said that you've disgraced yourself so badly that he can no longer think of you as his son."

"Hey, are you listening to me?"—Kikue's voice. Takashi opened his eyes. She was standing beside the cot, looking down at him. "Hey, are you going to get up?" she demanded, folding her arms. Desire fluttered in the back of his mind; he knew vaguely that he had wanted Kikue only moments ago, but the ardor itself was gone, the giddy expectation subsumed in a thick, heavy torpor. Briefly, he tried to rouse himself but, ah, that dress of hers looked like too much trouble to remove; sleep, on the other hand, beckoned like a naked, easy lover. He closed his eyes again.

Kikue's voice echoed distantly, as if she were calling down to him standing at the bottom of an empty well: "Hey, are you falling asleep? You can't sleep here . . . wake up . . . wake up . . . oh damn. . . ." Then the mouth of the well seemed to close, and he was left in darkness and silence.

• • •

Face of a Stranger

Kogoro ran through the dark streets in terror and dismay. His left foot skidded as he planted it squarely in a pile of dog shit; he scarcely noticed and lumbered on. What was dog shit to a man who was wont to till his manure-covered fields in bare feet, after all? A crisp wind was blowing and he had no coat on, and yet his shirt was drenched with sweat. His crumpled hat teetered uncertainly on his head, twice falling off as he ran. His eyes bulged open as wide as his thick, drooping lids would allow. Gusts of hot steam billowed out of his slack, half-open mouth. The streets were deserted, save for a small stray dog yapping at him from a distance. When Kogoro came within ten feet, the dog turned tail and fled.

What a disaster. He had been caught. Kogoro's ears burned and his flesh crawled with an overweening shame—shame not for his own sake, but for Kikue's. He had ruined their secret, exposed her. The scorn that he had endured all his life would now come down on her head once it became known that she had been with him—oh, God—alone, in her hut.

Kogoro stumbled to a halt. He bent over, clutching his knees and panting like a steam locomotive. For all his size, he cut a desolate figure. He wished he could burrow into the dirt like a worm. He wished he were dead. He wished, in fact, that he'd never been born.

From the very beginning, it seemed, he had been nothing but a source of pain and misfortune for others. His diminutive mother, barely four feet tall and no more than ninety-five pounds soaking wet, nearly died giving birth to her whopping fourteen-pound, twenty-two-inch-long infant; so hard was his delivery that it left her with a permanent limp and a bent-over back. At this ostensibly happy occasion Kogoro's father—who at five seven was the tallest member of his family—took one look at his newborn son and swore the monstrosity could not be his, and went so far as to accuse his wife of adultery, bestiality, communion with the devil, even as she lay bleeding, half-dead, and delirious with pain from twelve hours of labor. Naturally, at the time she was ill-disposed to listen to such remarks, and relations between them were never quite the same.

Kogoro dragged himself on, barely able to lift his blockish feet; his throat was raw, at once frozen and burning, from sucking in the cold night air. The muscles in his thick legs cramped and clutched; a stitch dug into his beefy side. He walked unsteadily, weaving lazy S's like a drunkard. After what seemed like hours, he reached his truck, which he had parked ten blocks away, and climbed in. When he sat down, he felt a lump in his back pocket and heard an expensive-sounding crunch: his watch. He didn't care. He just wanted to get home and fall into bed.

As he drove down the dark, narrow highway to his farm Kogoro tried not to remember anything, and after ten minutes he was able to forget Kikue and Takashi for a while. But in spite of himself his mind began to wander onto more dangerous terrain: his family back in Kunioku, a tiny, remote hamlet of about a hundred people on the Japan Sea coast. When he realized how badly he wanted to forget his own kin, he squeezed his eyes shut, blushing with shame. He opened them just in time to avoid running into a ditch. The truck fishtailed and teetered, but regained the road.

Kogoro glanced up at the rear-view mirror, which overflowed with the blurred reflection of his huge face. He considered his present situation: a man of means, an independent farmer, driving, actually driving, an American-made truck that was his biggest pride and thrill on a road in California, the United States of America. The unlikely confluence of events that landed him here was too dizzying to contemplate.

When he looked back at the road, he saw a pair of glowing eyes dead ahead. Before he could react, he heard a succession of sickening thuds underneath the truck. He pulled over and looked back. A skunk, with its body crushed, was bouncing its head against the pavement, writhing vainly to get up on its useless limbs. The muffled thumping evoked for him, strangely enough, the image of his mother gently patting his father on the back to quell one of his coughing fits near the end of his life. He wondered whether he might be able to help the animal somehow. Before he could get out of his truck, though, the thumping ceased and the animal lay still. Kogoro shuddered, then got back on the road, driving barely five miles per hour.

A rancid odor permeated the cab, making his eyes water and nearly causing him to gag. He did not attribute the smell to the carrion, though. Even his truck, his prized truck, was a source of disaster, he thought, chagrined: he could not accomplish a task as simple as driving down a desolate, moonlit road without doing harm. No, the stink, he was certain, came from him—it was the odor of his shame, which clung to him like contagion all the way from Japan to America.

four

Takashi woke to the grainy light floating in through the window of Kikue's hut. He felt refreshed, even purified, by hours of unbroken sleep. Unlike the first time, he knew where he was; the only mystery was *how long*. That gap in time—it might have been six hours or six weeks, for all he knew—made him impatient to start the day.

As soon as his feet hit the floor, he noticed that he was wearing someone else's clothes—a woodcutter's, from the looks of them. The shabby rags reeked of mildew and age and looked as if they might fall off like dead leaves off a tree at the slightest tremor. Curious, he fiddled with the coarse twine holding up his tattered britches, and searched for his own clothes. But the room was bare save for a pair of calcified-looking wooden clogs standing by the door.

69

He slipped them on and stepped out the door—to behold a desolate China Alley. All of the huts looked abandoned, their windows empty and doors flung open. Nothing moved, not even the air.

Takashi wondered what had become of the denizens until a pang of hunger seized his stomach. He felt as if he hadn't eaten in days. The cramps tightened steadily, forcing him to hunch over. He forgot all about the abandoned huts or his odd clothes; food was all that mattered to him now.

Without a thought he walked out of the alley and into the business district. There was no one in sight. He kept walking a straight line to the town limits, then quit the town proper and continued along the coastal road that led to the outlying farmland of the county. Some hidden impulse seemed to be guiding him.

After an hour of steady walking he paused and turned around: the terrain was not at all familiar. He looked down at his feet: even the road was gone. Wind rustled through the tall grass, and he noted that he was standing in a meadow. Thoroughly disoriented, he spun wildly, looking out in all directions. Then he stopped abruptly and stumbled back two steps.

A large mansion with a gold roof, built in the manner of a feudal castle, stood not more than twenty yards in front of him. Takashi scratched his head—how could he have missed such a monstrosity? He noticed the gates to the courtyard were open, and he peered through them for any signs of life, but there was no one about. Another cramp dug into his side, spurring him onward. He ambled casually toward the gates, his hopes rising

Yoji Yamaguchi

with each step. Surely, he thought, the owners would not begrudge poor Takashi a bite to eat.

As he walked through the gates he could hear the chattering of birds. He crept diffidently through the wide, dusty courtyard, expecting to be challenged at any moment. But the place seemed empty.

"*Irrashaimase.*" A woman's voice behind him caused Takashi to cry out in alarm. He whirled around and nearly tripped over his own heels.

She was young, maybe seventeen or eighteen, and of such stunning beauty she scarcely seemed real, dressed in a brilliant blue-green kimono of expensive silk, embroidered with an intricate pattern of cranes in various attitudes. She studied him with a mild curiosity and asked: "What is it you're looking for?"

Without question she was the most beautiful woman Takashi had ever seen. The chance of a lifetime! he thought feverishly, and his mind reeled as he tried to think of a reply that would charm her off her feet. But after a moment of anguished silence that seemed like hours to him, he could only blurt out stupidly: "Uhn?" His tongue felt like a dead eel stuffed in his maw.

To his immense relief, she smiled at him kindly. "Why have you come to my home?" she asked, her voice all patience.

"Eh, ah, I was just taking a walk . . . and I . . . noticed the gate was open," Takashi stammered, trying to sound nonchalant. He didn't dare let on that he was starving.

The woman stared at him with a smile fixed on her face. Takashi glanced down and his breath caught in panic: he had forgotten about his bumpkin's clothes. How could he explain

Face of a Stranger

his costume without sounding like a crackpot? He broke out in a cold sweat.

She did not seem to notice. "Well, in any case, I'm glad you've come. Perhaps you might do me a favor?"

"Uhn? I mean, sure!" he exclaimed. He would have crawled through fire for her at that moment. "Ehh—what can I do?"

"I must go out for a few hours. Unfortunately, there is no one but me to watch the house. Could you stay here while I'm gone?"

Takashi could scarcely believe his luck: this beautiful woman living alone in a splendid mansion! And all he had to do was stand guard for a few hours—who knew what might happen? "Of course! No problem! You can count on me!"

"Thank you. Now follow me, please." She led him to the main house and into a large antechamber with mahogany walls and floor that shined like ice. "Perhaps you would like something to eat?" A sumptuous meal of assorted fishes, pheasant, vegetables delicately carved, and a heaping bowl of rice lay waiting for him on an ebony serving tray.

He could barely restrain himself. "Oh well, sure. It looks delicious," he muttered with thinly feigned indifference. As badly as he wanted the woman, he could hardly wait for her to leave him to his food. He deposited himself on a plump pillow and stared at the feast before him.

The woman said: "I'll be on my way now. But I must ask you not to leave this room while I am gone. You must not enter any other room in the house." Her voice sounded ominous.

"Understood," he murmured. When he finally tore his eyes

away from the food she was already gone. He shrugged, then happily commenced to gorge himself.

After polishing off enough food for three, Takashi felt oddly dissatisfied—in fact, his stomach felt no fuller than before. He ruefully contemplated the empty dishes and thought: what now? The idea of sitting alone in that empty room for hours was almost too tiresome to contemplate.

He began to wonder about the woman's injunction: how could he be expected to guard the house if he was restricted to one room? And how could she leave him all alone and trust him not to start roaming the halls? The giddiness he had felt in her luminous presence began to fade. Suspicion set in. Perhaps she was testing him—his trustworthiness or, even worse, his servility.

That has to be it, Takashi thought indignantly: she wants me under her thumb! Why, she was probably still in the house, hiding somewhere and spying on him through a peephole. The feeling of eyes upon him made his skin crawl. He froze.

Finally he could stand it no longer and leapt to his feet. He resolved to find the woman and confront her. He stormed out of the antechamber and found himself in a long, dimly lit corridor lined with four doors.

He came upon the first door and slid it open. Inside were three maids cleaning the room. When they saw him their faces froze in terror and, in an instant, they vanished before his eyes.

Shaken, Takashi pulled the door shut and hurried to the next room. It proved to be a stable with two stalls, occupied by a magnificent black stallion and a scrofulous, rheumy-eyed ass.

Face of a Stranger

In the third room Takashi saw a golden barrel dripping sake into a small ceramic jar. He crept in, grabbed the jar, and chugged down its contents. The jar, small enough to hold with one hand, seemed to have no bottom; sake flowed continuously until he nearly gagged. He let the jar drop to the floor and staggered out.

By the time he reached the last room, Takashi could barely stand. The paper and wood door felt as if it were made of iron. He pushed it open, straining every muscle, took one step inside, and fell to his knees.

The room looked as big as the entire mansion. The ceiling was a good three stories high; the walls were painted royal blue. In one corner stood a golden screen. At the far end of the room a man and a woman sat on a raised dais. The man was dressed in a black robe, the woman in white.

Takashi tried to stand, but his legs were useless. So he crawled the length of the floor to the dais, flopped onto his side, and curled up, fetallike, panting heavily.

The couple, both gray-haired, in late middle age, looked down at him with disdain. "Once again, you've disappointed," the man sighed.

Takashi tried to sit up, but his head felt like it was made of stone. "Eh? What's that?" he snarled from the floor.

The man reached inside his sleeve and produced a small bird's nest containing three round, thumb-size blue eggs. He picked up one and rolled it lightly between his fingers, then tossed it to the floor. A tiny bird flew out from the wreckage and disappeared. He dashed the second egg to the floor, hatching another bird, and then the third, with the same result.

From behind the screen the beautiful woman of the mansion came running out. Her hair was undone and hopelessly tangled, and dark circles ringed her wide, frantic eyes. As she ran her kimono billowed behind her like giant wings.

"Oh my children, my poor children!" she wailed as she stood over Takashi. She pointed a trembling finger at him and ranted: "You broke your word! I told you not to go beyond the first room! You can't be counted on to do the smallest thing! Now my children are gone and it's your fault!" She ran toward the door, wailing. Two seconds later the room was silent. Takashi looked up to see that she was already gone.

His head dropped to the floor and he rubbed his eyes with his fists. "I must be drunk again," he muttered.

"Do you know who that was?" the man asked severely.

"I don't even know who you are!" Takashi raged. He writhed, trying to regain his feet.

"Why, Big Brother, don't you recognize me? It's Keichi." The man thrust his pasty, jowly face forward.

"Keichi? What are you talking about? That's my kid brother! Ha ha ha! Come on, what's going on here?"

The man shook his head in pity. "Takashi-kun, don't you recognize our home?"

Takashi looked around: they were in his father's Western-style study. The man was seated at his father's desk while the woman stood behind him. Takashi was sitting in a straight-back chair opposite them, and clutched its arms in terror. Then he noticed a trivial detail that enraged him.

75

Face of a Stranger

"Those are my clothes you're wearing!" he cried. He wondered how they fit the portly fellow.

"Keichi" ignored him and said: "That unfortunate woman, you see, would have been your wife if you hadn't gotten yourself kicked out of the house. And the three little chicks were, well, I think you know . . ." He shrugged and held up his hands.

Takashi mumbled in a semistupor: "The mansion . . ."

"Ah, that would have been yours as well. You see, the woman was from an old and distinguished family, of considerably higher station than ours. Yet they suffered from financial difficulty and, worse, lacked a male heir. While you were in middle school Father had already begun making plans: you were to have married the daughter and they in turn were to adopt you, thereby cementing a bond between our two households—"

"Tell me something I don't already know," Takashi snapped.

"But your unseemly behavior and untold embarrassments thwarted Father's goal; the other family declined the match even before any formal offers were made. Father explained all of this to me shortly before he passed away."

Takashi hesitated. "Passed away?"

"Yes—four years after you left for America. I was going to send you a telegram, but Mother forbade it—not that she really expected you to show up. So now I am running the household, with my wife, Mariko." He waved his hand toward the the slender, elegant-looking older woman standing behind him.

"Mariko?" Takashi struggled to recall the name. "You mean the Ayabes' fat little girl? Her?"

Yoji Yamaguchi

To his surprise, she stuck out her tongue and sneered: "Oh, yeah? I'm better looking than that old whore you sleep with. Ha!" She and Keichi started giggling uncontrollably.

Takashi's head was spinning when it occurred to him: if Keichi and Mariko were grown up, then he . . . For the first time, he noticed that his hands were gnarled and scaly, and his forearms looked like shriveled reeds. He reached up to grab his hair and came up empty; when he rubbed his shiny pate he howled in anguish. The couple taunted him, laughing and chanting a singsong ditty:

> "Old Man, Old Man,
> you're all alone;
> your wife is gone,
> your kids have flown.
> Old Man, Old Man,
> you're on your own."

Takashi could bear it no longer. He covered his ears with his hands and doubled over. Finally the laughter and the singing stopped.

He looked up and saw that he was standing in the meadow once again. The mansion was gone. In the distance he could hear a bird singing—or was it a woman crying?

Takashi woke in the darkened hut, clammy with sweat and breathing hard. His throat was parched. The window was battened down; light seeped in around its edges and through the cracks in the walls. The familiar oily smell of the kerosene lamp, the moldy tang rising from the cold, hard mattress brought him to his senses.

The air was dank. He shivered and rubbed his arms, trying to warm himself. His head was spinning, and his body felt as brittle as dry wood. Slowly, he slithered out of bed and stumbled to the door. When he pulled it open, he was nearly blinded by the deluge of midday sunlight.

He was supposed to have been at work at six-thirty sharp. An awful vision swelled in his already aching head, of everything that he had left undone, the chaos at the Warren house that must have ensued while he slept on Kikue's rack.

The Warrens had made it clear his first day on the job that tardiness would be grounds for immediate dismissal. Takashi had no doubt that he would be fired. What excuse could he give them, after all—that he'd overslept in a brothel? *Beikoku Rodo Benran* offered no instruction on plausible lies in English.

As always, China Alley looked like a squalid ghost town during the day. The shabby stillness of the empty lane made him feel excluded, cast out, adrift. He turned up the collar of his coat and dug his hands in his pockets. It seemed to him that everyone in the world was somewhere where they belonged, while he stood alone with nowhere to go and in no hurry to get there.

The thought of being dismissed yet again, by two *hakujin* he despised more than any, galvanized Takashi—and inspired in him an idea. Since he was as good as gone, he would proceed to their home directly and quit on the spot, without notice or apologies or excuses. No, he would not suffer the indignity of dismissal, not by them. All servile niceties he would cast aside, to stand up, unflinching, and fling defiance in their rotten brown teeth—but not before demanding his back pay. He threw back his shoulders and clenched his fists. The magnitude of what he was about to do almost moved him to tears. He sneezed instead.

Buoyed by his own ingenuity, heady with his newfound purpose—and still unsteady from the flu—Takashi set out like a man going off to war. All of the slights he had suffered came rushing back, whetting his anger into a cold, keen edge. His clothes were rumpled and stained with sweat. To hell with it! he thought. The rougher he looked, the better. This was a war, after all—a war not only for his honor, but for all Issei domestics humiliated by their *hakujin* bosses. He emerged from China Alley and marched through the bustling streets of the business district with a terrible resolve.

Takashi brushed through throngs of people, strutting with a cocksure gait, his hands in his pockets and a sneer on his face. He bumped into a passerby and paid no heed to his complaint. Weaving left and right, he walked directly into the path of an elderly woman who looked up into his face and asked: "Excuse me, sir, but are you all right?" He ignored her and walked on. The aspersions of these idle, silly people did not faze him. He was resolute.

It was almost two o'clock. The thought of the havoc he had created with his absence no longer alarmed but rather delighted him. They would see how valuable he was, he thought gleefully.

He pictured a kitchen in shambles, rotting food attracting swarms of flies; the windows cloudy with soot; and Woodrow rabid, foaming at the mouth. He quickened his pace. His head was spinning with elation.

Takashi had not eaten all day. By the time he turned the corner to Garfield Street, where the Warrens lived, he was exhausted. As he dragged himself up to the gray and white Queen Anne house, he could see a man, dressed in a white suit identical to his, sweeping the walk furiously. "Oi," Takashi called out brusquely, "dare ka?" His throat felt as if he had swallowed hot sand; he broke down coughing.

The fellow whirled around, startled. He was young, sixteen or so, rangy and long-faced. "What are you doing here?" Takashi demanded.

The boy gawked at him. "My n-name is . . . is . . . Ishikawa," he stammered. "I . . . w-w-work here."

"Kugakusei ka?"

"H-h-hai."

Takashi surveyed the house. It had not, as he had hoped, fallen to wrack and ruin in his absence; it looked as it always had and, he suspected, always would, long after they were all gone—him, the old women, Woodrow, Ishikawa. For a moment he felt as if he had never been there before. Takashi understood now: whether he stayed or left, nothing changed. The old women didn't care what had happened to him; they simply replaced him as easily as one replaces a button on a shirt, a lace on a shoe. He realized he would be getting no satisfaction—or money.

Yoji Yamaguchi

Though he had no reason to stay, Takashi did not want to leave just yet. "So how long have you been working here?" he asked Ishikawa amicably.

Ishikawa gave him a sidelong glance, puzzled by the change in his demeanor, and resumed his sweeping. "Actually, I just started today. It seems the houseboy who used to work here didn't report for work. No notice, no explanation—he just didn't show. Probably skipped town. So the owners hired me on the spot. Can you believe it?"

Takashi rather enjoyed being incognito, hearing himself described in the third person. He decided to string the boy along. "You sure were lucky," he said admiringly, wiping his brow.

Ishikawa stopped sweeping and cocked his head. "Yes, I am, I suppose, but you know, it really burns me up—I mean, that guy walking off the job like that. What a bum! Men like him just make it harder for the rest of us. All it takes is one bad example like that to convince the hakujin not to hire any of us. Luckily, my bosses are fair people. They didn't hold another man's failings against me."

"Um, maybe he had a good excuse. Maybe he was sick or something," Takashi muttered before sneezing.

"I don't care if he was at death's door; there's no excuse for what he did. I mean, what good is a worker who's too sick to work?"

Takashi resisted the urge to grab the broom and thrash the fellow with it. The game no longer amused him. "Maybe he just couldn't take it anymore—I mean, being treated like a maid,

81

doing woman's work all day. It must be tough on a *man,*" he sneered.

Ishikawa didn't notice the snub. He recommenced his sweeping and said: "Yes, it is tough—a lot tougher than most people think! But the way I see it, work's work, and sometimes if you want to climb high, you have to crawl low first.

"After all, this is their country. We're newcomers, and in no position to pick and choose our lots in life here. We have to take what we can get and make the most of it. Maybe the ones who come after us will get to the top. But not if people refuse hard work and walk off their jobs like that no-account before me. Then we'll never get anywhere."

Ishikawa's platitudes made Takashi want to spit on the tidy, newly swept walk, but his mouth was bone dry. He tried to picture the young boy six months into the future; would his self-righteous optimism hold up under the humiliation and drudgery that awaited him? The thought of Ishikawa's inevitable comeuppance brought a furtive smile to Takashi's face.

But his satisfaction was short-lived; inexplicably, he felt a pang of sadness for the boy. And for himself as well: what could he look forward to in this country? Another house, another white suit? Was a broom the promised end for them all?

Inside the house, Woodrow began barking vehemently. Takashi recognized the tone; it meant a stranger was about. It took a moment for him to realize that the stranger was him. The door opened and there stood an old woman, gray-haired, dumpy, hump-backed, standing uncertainly on her spindly legs. Which one was it? He could not tell.

82

It hardly mattered. At once Takashi was filled with an intense loathing. He wanted to blame her for everything—his flu, his poverty, his haunting dream, even Kikue's unenviable lot. She (Joan? Jane?) was no longer simply a churlish, fussy old woman, but the *Hakujin*, the White Devil, embodiment and root cause of all their suffering.

The old resolve, the old grandeur, came back in an instant, swelling up into his throat, nearly moving him to tears. He would avenge himself, all of them, for all they had to endure. He would be a hero.

She called out in a wheezy voice: "Charlie?"

"Hai," both men chirped in unison, then stared at each other, surprised.

Face of a Stranger

five

"The things I do for Kikue," Shino grumbled as she tied knots in the straps of the short red dress to keep them from slipping off her bony shoulders. The tassels on the bust line lay immobile, plastered against her flat chest. Because the hideous-looking thing was a gift from the man she was about to see, she had to wear it. She stepped into a pair of slippers and opened the door to her hut, checking in both directions to see if stupid Junzo was about. Satisfied that the coast was clear, she slipped out noiselessly and hurried off.

Kato's gambling den was housed on the second floor of Koyama's bathhouse, but a stone's throw from China Alley. The proximity served him well, a boon for his comfort trade. Here Kato was wise, understanding full well the stimulating effect gambling had on winners and losers alike. It was not difficult to funnel his clientele from his tables to his beds.

Shino pushed the door open. It led to a steep, narrow flight of stairs, sagging and bare, dimly lit by a single bulb. As she ascended, she became quickly short of breath, partly from the severity of the incline, but more from an apprehension that seized her without warning. What am I doing here? she wondered, thinking first of the gambling den in particular, then of America in general. She stopped on the uppermost stair. For a panicked instant her memory fled her, and she felt suspended in that place, that moment, cut off from all she perceived around her.

The stale air was heavy and overbearing and the dim shadows seemed to thicken. The dull clamor of the gaming tables emanating from behind the door to her left sounded miles away. She looked down at the steps and flexed her knees slightly, pressing her weight down on her soles, to feel the warped, grainy pinewood, how solid it was. She touched the wall; it was cool, and the smooth wood felt reassuring to her fingers.

She stepped to the door and knocked thrice. It was a plain wooden door with a looking slot—at eye level for an average man, but nearly half a foot above her head. There was no response. She knocked again. The shutter slid open and a pair of thick-lidded eyes stared out at her. "Nan dai?" the voice behind the door asked gruffly—a teenager, from the sound of it.

"I'm looking for Saigo."

"No Saigo here. You got the wrong place," the voice said perfunctorily.

Yoji Yamaguchi

"Please, it's important."

"Who are you?" The eyes narrowed.

"Shino."

The eyes relaxed. As he stared at her impassively, the uncanny feeling Shino had felt minutes before returned when she considered how she was talking to a pair of eyes in a door. Briefly, she felt the urge to run headlong down the stairs to daylight, where all was normal. But where would that place be? She studied the door, every inch of it save the looking slot; like the steps, its solidity calmed her.

The boy blinked, and he grunted what sounded like "Wait." The peephole slid shut. A minute later the slot abruptly opened again. A different pair of eyes peered out at her, wider than the first pair and sharper in their gaze. When she heard a voice ask "What is it?" she knew it was Saigo.

Shino said as casually as she could: "Hey, chief, I need to talk."

"Go on," Saigo said coolly.

"Can I come in?"

"Here's fine."

"I hear the boss lost some of his luggage," she said.

Saigo grunted as he stared at her red dress.

"Cost him a lot of money, I hear."

Saigo's eyes dipped below the slot and Shino found herself staring at his forehead. She heard a loud slurp of noodles being eaten. "Uhn," he grunted, his voice muffled.

"What's he going to do about it?"

Saigo snorted, and Shino detected a glint of derision in his eyes. "Usually we'd just bribe the right people and that'd be the end of it; but this one would take a fortune to clean up."

"So what's going to happen?"

"What's it to you?" he demanded.

Shino shrugged. "Just curious. What's her name?"

"Kuruzaki something-or-other. Someone want her?"

"Didn't say that. Where's she from?"

"From Nara . . . no, wait. She's from Kobe. This guy a pimp, or some sucker looking for a bride?"

"Who?"

"Whoever it was who sent you. You think I don't know what you're up to? You can't fool me."

"Wouldn't think of it. How old is she?"

"Seventeen. You think you're smart, don't you?"

"Not at all. I hear this girl . . . what's her name again?"

"Kuruzaki."

"I hear she's beautiful."

Saigo cocked an eyebrow. "Could be. Could be not."

"What's that mean?"

"I mean, I'm not telling you anything. You're too nosy for your own good."

Shino sniffed. "I think you really mean you don't know what you're talking about."

Saigo blinked. "What d'ya mean?"

"You don't know what this girl looks like."

"I do so! I've seen her picture."

"I bet she's a sow."

"Not at all! She's better looking than any of you lousy whores."

Yoji Yamaguchi

"Ha! She's probably hairy and missing teeth. Stinks, too, I bet."

"What do you know!" Saigo fumed.

"Neh, I think your whole story is shit. I bet the boss got taken, paying Oshichi top dollar for a two-bit carcass, and now he doesn't want to let anyone see his mistake. So he's leaving her out on that island, hiding her," Shino sneered. "And I bet her name isn't even Kuruzaki!"

"It is, dammit!" Saigo bellowed. "And she's a real beauty, too! Just like I said!"

"Yeah, just like Oshichi promised Kato that Haru would be his favorite," Shino taunted. "'Course she didn't say it was because she looks just like him." She held out her arms to suggest Haru's girth, and laughed gaily.

"You don't know anything!" Saigo roared. "I have the girl's file right here! I've seen it; you haven't!"

"So let's see it!"

"Wait!" The peephole slammed shut, and Shino could hear him storming away. Giddy with the sense of her own power, she marveled at her ability to winnow gold from flax, and at the stupidity of all men. What fools they are! she thought merrily.

The door opened and Saigo stepped out. Lean as a knife, with a fat, shiny scar beneath his right eye, he seemed to loom over Shino, even though he was only four inches taller than her. He handed her a packet. "Go ahead. See for yourself."

She opened it and quickly read through the contents, repeating the data silently to herself, willing herself to remember it all:

Face of a Stranger

name, birth date, place of birth, residence, names of the girl's parents, father's occupation, names of her primary and middle schools.

"Satisfied?" Saigo asked.

"Umm," Shino murmured and read on. The copiousness of the file began to annoy her. Why does Kato need to know all of this? she thought. It wasn't as if he was going to marry her; and besides, he gave them phony papers and identities to bring them into the country anyway. She supposed that he needed to know all about someone in order to truly own her; she wondered if her own life had been similarly dissected, and guessed that it had, making her all the more cross.

Then she pulled out the girl's picture: a recent one, from the looks of it, probably paid for by Oshichi herself. Saigo's protestations had hardly done her justice; she was the most beautiful woman Shino had ever seen. A pang—maybe of jealousy or desire, or both, she couldn't tell—seized her, leaving her disoriented, flustered. She was so captivated by the luminous face that she did not notice the gleam in Saigo's eyes.

A tattoo of a white dog on his right bicep caught her eye, then a flash of his hard, wiry body, before he was all over her. "C'mon, you've wasted enough of my time," he grunted. He grabbed her around the waist and pinned her against the wall, forcing his leg between her thighs. "I'm pretty smart, too, eh?" he panted in her ear.

His face, only inches above hers, looked enormous, and for an instant she could see her reflection in his pupils—white, hazy shadows on black, abysmal pools. She shut her eyes. His

Yoji Yamaguchi

hot, sour breath coursed over her face, stinking of red pepper and beer. As he hiked up her dress, she braced herself, wishing for that faraway feeling she'd had moments before to return, and thought: The things I do for Kikue.

Masajiro Inada walked slowly back to his hotel, his mind heavy with foreboding. He was in no rush to tell his wife the news; he rather felt like a schoolboy delivering a note from his teacher to his parents, not knowing how they would react and fearing the worst.

He had just come from a meeting with the Reverend Onara and two parishioners, Mrs. Hayashi and Mrs. Urusaki, to discuss the letter Onara had received from Katherine Maurer, the famous missionary who worked with new arrivals on Angel Island. In it, she wrote of a Japanese woman who was being held in solitary confinement on the island.

Her name is Hana Kuruzaki. She is a young girl, perhaps seventeen or so and extraordinarily beautiful. From what I can gather, she is also quite intelligent and perceptive, though her advent to these shores—smuggled like contraband aboard a freighter, her destination a brothel—has left her bewildered and suspicious. Because she has been treated here like a criminal rather than the victim of an unscrupulous panderer, she is distrustful of Americans in general— hence, I believe, her antagonism toward me.

I fear also that her mind is not wholly sound. Not only has she steadfastly rejected my ministering, to the point of

91

feigning sleep whenever I try to read to her from the Good Book, she has taken to behaving in a most base and vulgar manner. Her clothes and her very bearing suggest a refined background; yet, in her distraction she is wont to eat with her hands, belch loudly, use profane language when angry.

Today, the most extraordinary thing occurred. She was interviewed by an American immigration official, who would have undoubtedly recommended sending her back to Japan and her family—had he heard the truth. But I was told by one of the Chinese women in my mission, who was on hand for the interview, that the translator got Miss Kuruzaki's Japanese all wrong, distorting and changing her answers utterly, so that her story sounded perfectly unexceptional; through his dissembling he even explained why she was found hiding in the cargo hold. The translator was either ridiculously incompetent, or else he had his own agenda. I suspect the latter. It would not surprise me if Mr. Furukawa from the Japanese consulate had prevailed upon him to perpetrate this fraud; when Furukawa tried to interview Miss Kuruzaki himself she had treated him saucily and sent him away.

So now she will be allowed to enter the country—but to what end? Will the panderer be waiting to take her away to his brothel? That simply cannot be.

As I said, she has spurned all of my tenders of assistance. She will not trust any Caucasian, I am certain. So I ask you in the name of our Lord Jesus Christ to take this unfortunate woman into your fold, protect her, nourish her, and show her

*the best of Christian charity. I will give you the exact time of
her release, &c. &c. . . .*

There was no question whether they should agree; but
Reverend Onara tempered their enthusiasm. "Our mission for
fallen women is full to capacity. There is no room for her there."

"But how can that be?" Mrs. Hayashi asked.

"It would seem that none of the women want to leave. We
already have a waiting list for beds."

When the other three turned to Inada he blushed. He knew
what they wanted; he also knew they would not be so crude as
to ask him outright to put the woman up in his hotel. Silently,
they waited for him to offer.

But he did not want to. Business was finally beginning to
pick up, and it was hardly the time to fill up one of his vacant
rooms with a nonpaying guest; he supposed he would have to
feed her as well. . . . He stopped, dismayed by his parsimony
and selfishness.

And his disingenuousness. He knew the true reason for his
reluctance. His arrangement with Kikue had been the subject
of much speculation and innuendo among the congregation,
and even at that moment he could see its effects in their eyes.
Because Kikue never deigned to set foot in their church, his
story of providing sanctuary for her was met with skepticism.
He was seen by many as a libertine, keeping a concubine
under the same roof with his family, under the pretense of
reforming her; Sumiko, his wife, was cast as a paragon of
patience.

He stopped in his tracks and winced; the pain of remembering the day Kikue moved in was still palpable.

"You pig!" Sumiko screamed. "I bet you had this planned all along! You were keeping this room warm for your little whore! Well, she's here now, but I warn you: if I catch you sniffing around up here. . . . "

And yet Inada began to wonder more and more whether Sumiko was not secretly pleased at having Kikue in the hotel—and thus having a ready cudgel to beat his brow at will. She was quick to end all disputes by alluding to "the whore" (and, if she was feeling especially rancorous, insulting his mother as well). Inada had begun to feel that he was being blackmailed as much by his own wife as by the prostitute.

Of course, he had to admit, Sumiko had always been rather on the contrary side—long before Kikue had insinuated herself into their lives. Were it not for her dogged insistence on joining him in America before he was ready, after all, he might not be in the fix he was in now.

And now he had no choice but to take in yet another of Kato's women. He could not bear to imagine the calumny that would ensue were he to turn her away even as he let Kikue stay. And besides, he consoled himself, it is the right thing to do.

"Shikata ga nai," he murmured to himself as he proceeded on. "Sometimes the just person gets what is due the unjust, and the unjust what is due the just." The words of Ecclesiastes soothed him.

He stopped again. This is not futility, but punishment, he corrected himself: I have brought these troubles upon myself.

Yoji Yamaguchi

Yet, he was still not certain exactly how. One visit to a whore? Helping himself to her money? None of these seemed to warrant the indignities he had to suffer. He recited another verse: "God has so ordered the world that no man can discover the true meaning of things." But that was cold comfort. Oh, he had embraced his new religion with his heart and soul, but still sometimes it did not make much sense to him.

There was more. Of late, Sumiko had been especially forward after receiving a letter from her younger brother Imoyaro, who was working in an Alaskan fish cannery. Apparently the Issei workers there had organized and were staging a general strike; Sumiko had no doubt that they would all be fired and left to fend for themselves in this foreign land.

"What will he do? He's only sixteen; he can't speak any English. What will my poor baby brother do?" Sumiko sighed more than once, always loud enough for her husband to hear.

Inada knew full well what he would do: arrive at their door with hat in hand. This he could not allow. Coarse, ill-mannered, stupid enough to drive one to distraction, Imoyaro was one of those people who regarded succor from others as his birthright. Worse, he and Sumiko were slavishly devoted to each other. Living with both of them would be far worse than anything Kikue might do to him.

Inada wondered how Sumiko would respond to Hana Kuruzaki. The fact that Reverend Onara was supporting the girl might assuage his wife's suspicions. Would that I had never seen a prostitute before, and may I never see another one again, he thought wearily as his hotel came into view.

Face of a Stranger

• • •

Shino walked with an attitude, head cocked back, arms swinging to the rhythm of her long, brusque strides. She could still smell Saigo, feel his hands on her skin, feel him inside her, but it didn't mean a thing. She was on her way to see Kikue.

Once she entered the business district on J Street, Shino began to feel the stares, hear the murmurs of dismay and disapproval, around her. Two well-dressed women walked toward her on the sidewalk, brazenly curling their lips and clucking as they passed by. Shino wanted to turn around and shout: *Go fuck yourselves*. Instead, she put them out of her mind and walked on. She had more important things to worry about.

Still, she was seething when she arrived at the Pacific Hotel, and fairly stormed through the front door. As she entered the narrow foyer leading to the front desk, she could smell the faint aroma of bread; muffled voices were emanating from the doorway to her right. She stopped and looked in to see twelve men sitting at a long table, their heads bowed and their hands clasped before them, while the food sat on the table untouched. They stumbled through a song in English that made no sense to her:

"Praise God from Whom all blessings flow;
Praise Him all creatures here below;
Praise Him above our Heavenly Host;
Praise Father, Son, and Holy Ghost . . . "

"Eh, chotto gomen," she called out brightly, throwing the ceremony into turmoil. The twelve men looked up at her and leapt

96

out of their chairs—some kicking theirs over in consternation—mouths agape and faces blanched with dismay and confusion. All was silent as they gawked at her, dumbstruck.

Shino was annoyed. "What's the matter with you guys? Haven't you ever seen a woman before?" They remained transfixed, their expressions reminding her of freshly caught fish. She began to feel mischievous. "Here, take a good look," she said, hiking the hem of her short dress even higher. "Hooohhh," the men gasped.

"What are you doing here?" a woman's voice barked from the end of the foyer.

Shino dropped her dress and turned to see a short, dumpy woman scowling at her. She had on a faded brown sack of a dress that hung down to her ankles and made her look amorphous; Shino couldn't tell if the white apron she was wearing was tied around her waist or her chest. For such a rotund woman, she had a surprisingly taut, leathery face. Shino, who feared no one, could not help but step back. "What makes you think you can come in here, peddling yourself in that disgraceful outfit? This is a respectable hotel—no place for the likes of you. Get out of here! Take your abominable business elsewhere, slut, whore, strumpet!" She approached menacingly. Shino knew by now that she was face-to-face with none other than Mrs. Inada.

Normally, she would have been more than happy to go at it tooth and nail with anyone who dared to talk to her like that. But when she glanced into the dining room and noticed the twelve men huddled on the far side of the room, behind the

97

table, she thought better of it. "No, no, you've got it wrong," she said, placatingly. "I'm not trying to pick up these men; I'm here to see someone." She noticed the twelve men turning their backs to her, afraid to watch what might happen next.

To Shino's relief, Mrs. Inada turned on her heel and marched to the staircase at the end of the hallway. "Masajiro! Masajiro!" she howled as she bounded up the steps.

Moments later Inada came running down, a baffled look on his face. He approached Shino and greeted her with a curt bow. "I am Inada," he introduced himself formally. "How might I be, ah, of service?"

Shino's resolve was beginning to waver. The whole business was turning out to be more trouble than she had bargained for; she wondered whether Arai was really worth it. How easy it would be to simply turn and run out the door and never look back.

But no: the memories of Arai walking away from her that night in the alley seized her like a hand clutching her heart. And besides, she reasoned, she did not give herself to Saigo in a dark hallway, then come all this way and stand toe-to-toe with a mad woman, just to be turned away. She was committed; might as well go for broke.

But first she decided to have a little fun. Without warning, she flopped to the floor, prostrating herself at Inada's feet, and wept with as much bitterness as she could muster. Inada jumped back in fright. "Oh, please forgive me!" she wailed. "I know I am nothing but a low-down common whore, unfit to set foot in your house. I was so desperate, I didn't know what else to do!" She sniffed for effect. "But I figured if anyone could help me, it would be you. Everybody knows what a virtuous, generous man you are, always ready to help others, especially poor helpless women like me." She peeked up and caught Inada with a stricken look on his face. It was hard for her not to grin.

Emboldened, Shino rose to her knees. "My name is Shino," she murmured. "I was brought over to this country by a treacherous man who tricked my parents with phony promises of marriage, and forced into this life of shame." Her voice cracked, a fortuitous accident, but also something of a surprise. Why get so choked up on her very own story?

"Soo ka," Inada intoned, nodding sagely. "And now you wish to escape this man, reform your life. That is admirable. You are in luck: our church runs a mission for women such as—"

"That's not what I meant," she snapped without thinking, taking both of them aback. "Er, that is—I was hoping you'd put me up here."

Inada stared at her in amazement. "Not as a guest, of course," she hastily added, "but as an employee. I'm a good worker; I'll do anything you say. Anything." She looked up at him, straining her eyes open as wide as she could.

Inada blanched and stepped backward, waving his trembling hands as if to ward her off. "Um, no . . . er . . . ah . . . I can't help you . . . you'd better leave."

Shino was furious; the humor of her little joke had backfired. She sprang to her feet, catching Inada by surprise and nearly sending him on his back. "What? Why not? What's wrong with me? What's she got over me, anyway? She's old, I'm

99

young, and I got a much better body! See?" She began to slip the straps off her shoulders.

"Nooo!" Inada wailed. "Don't do that!" His hysterical reaction riled her all the more.

"What is it with you? You like it better with old hags?" she jeered. Then she glanced over his shoulder and inhaled sharply.

Mrs. Inada stood at the top of the stairs, looking like a boulder perched tenuously on a cliff, threatening disaster. She glared at the two of them.

"So, another whore in our hotel!" she bellowed, bouncing down the stairs. "Maybe she can have our room. That's it! We'll all move out and live on the street, so this whore can live in luxury just like the other one. You see what you've done? Oh, but don't worry about your daughters; they're young; living out in the cold won't hurt them."

"Sumiko . . . " Inada said in a weary voice.

"Look at the little tart, flaunting her body for all to see! A little while ago she was even propositioning our guests!"

That does it, Shino thought. "Oh ho," she sneered. "You think I'm so bad and you are all so good? You don't fool me. Go ni haitte go ni shitagae, neh. To live in America you have to act American, right? So you fellows bow to the hakujin god and do all the routines, the better to fit in."

"That's a lie! Our congregation is devout, one and all!" Mrs. Inada squealed.

"Really? Tell me, what does your religion have to say about fucking?"

Inada blushed furiously. "Fuck . . . er, fornication—especially

Yoji Yamaguchi

with a *prostitute*—we regard as a sin, an offense, a desecration of one's body, which God created in His own image, and is thus sacred," he declaimed.

"Well, whatever. So tell me this: if your fellows are so holy and upright, why are so many of them my best customers?"

Were not Inada standing between the two women, one can only imagine the outcome. He eyed them both warily as they glowered at each other.

"What is this?" It was Kikue, standing at the top of the stairs.

"Ah, you're here," Shino called out, genuinely pleased.

"Excuse me, but can my friend come up?" Kikue asked.

Inada, too, was visibly relieved. "Of course," he said, bowing.

Shino sidled past the couple, though not without favoring Mrs. Inada with a smirk. As she sprinted up the steps she burst into a fit of giggling, oblivious to Kikue's disapproving frown.

Once they were out of sight, Inada turned to his wife and clucked: "I must say that you did not set a very good example of the Christian way."

Mrs. Inada's jaw dropped. "You're a fine one to talk! And what kind of example do you set, doing business with whores, heathens, gamblers—the scum of the earth!"

"They are Japanese, and so are we," Inada said tersely. "Our faith does not change that. We have to stick together in this country."

"Oh, don't wave the flag at me! I know what's really important to you. As soon as somebody flashes money in your face, you're blind to everything else. Even though the Bible says you cannot serve God and mammon."

"It also says judge not lest ye be judged," he shot back. "Would you rather I let our daughters starve? Or maybe go working in the fields?"

"You even allow the heathen to practice their idolatry right here in our hotel—in front of the children."

"That again?" Inada asked. "Our guests were observing the emperor's birthday! What's wrong with that?"

"It is pagan idolatry. 'May the Son of Heaven reign ten thousand years.' There is only one Son of Heaven, and we bow to Him. Not that young boy."

"Sumiko! Show some respect! He is the emperor!"

"And we are in America."

"We're still Japanese!"

"We're Christians first."

Mrs. Inada scowled at her husband, then something behind him caught her eye. She stared in horror. Inada turned to see.

A dozen faces were peering out from the dining room door; all twenty-four eyes gazed at them, wide with fear and wonder. When their host and hostess turned toward them, the twelve men quickly ducked back out of sight.

Mr. and Mrs. Inada stared at each other in dismay, and he fumed at his wife: "Now look what you've done! You've embarrassed us in front of our guests with your shameful spectacle! Now I will have to make amends for your conduct!" That said, he scurried to the dining room and began to apologize with all the unction he could muster.

Mrs. Inada stood in the lobby. All was quiet; there were no traces, nothing left in the wake of the woman who had created

Yoji Yamaguchi

such havoc, as if she had merely been a ghostly apparition, an illusion that had appeared to all of them at once.

In the dining room, Tsushida, a troll-like old bachelor who was one of the most devout of their guests, hawked once and spoke in a reedy voice: "Inada-san."

"Hai," Inada answered with a flustered bow.

"Who was that young girl?"

"Ah, she is a poor wayward young woman who is trying to reform her life. She came to me for guidance."

"Ah, that is admirable." Tsushida nodded his head benevolently. Then he looked up at Inada and cracked a sunken, lipless grin that made his long, angular ears seem to slide up the sides of his acornlike head. "Ehh—I don't suppose she gave you her address, did she?"

"Old hag, am I?" Kikue said as Shino sat down on the bed facing her.

"What's that?" Shino mumbled. She was running her hands over the mattress, admiring its smoothness.

"I heard what you said."

"Uhn? Oh, no, I was talking about the bitch," she muttered, then craned her neck to examine the room. "What a place! I don't get it: why do you waste your time in the alley when you've got it made right here?"

"You think Kato would just let me walk away like that?"

"Huh—it'd take that shithead Junzo a year to figure out you were missing."

"I doubt it. Anyway, did you find out anything?"

Shino smiled and extracted the photo of Hana Kuruzaki. It was dog-eared, somewhat wrinkled, but otherwise intact. After Saigo had finished, she noticed the photo on the floor amid the scattered contents of the packet. While he fumbled with his trousers, his back turned to her, she had quickly snatched up the photo.

"How did you get this?" Kikue asked.

Shino pointed to the photo and said: "She's beautiful, isn't she? Show him her picture and Arai will be like a fish on a hook. And he'll die when he finds out that we tricked him, that she won't be his wife after all."

Kikue understood and did not press the matter. She looked at the photo. Yes, the girl was beautiful, though she was not as smitten by her as Shino clearly was. She looked up at her friend, who was craning her neck for another glimpse of the girl. "So. Tell me about her," Kikue said.

"Fifty-four, fifty-five, fifty-six . . . " The girl lay supine on the narrow wooden bench, spooning her left arm in a seamless arc while her legs fluttered to a steady rhythm. Her right arm lay still, wedged between her body and the wall. In the women's isolation room on the second floor of the immigration barracks—a closet, no more than five feet by six feet, stinking of new paint and green lumber, no light save that filtering through the latticed portal of the locked door—Hana Kuruzaki was practicing her backstroke.

"Sixty-nine, seventy, seventy-one . . . " she panted softly. Her right arm was falling asleep, and she feared that this unnatural technique would ruin her form. Still, it was with no small pride that she noticed how easily her slender body fit on the narrow bench.

For three weeks she had been locked up in that stuffy hole. Her meals—usually cabbage and rice, boiled to mush—were brought to her on a metal tray. Twice a day—morning and night—she was allowed out to use the bathroom, accompanied by one of the barracks matrons. This arrangement was her only consolation: because the Americans deemed her trouble, they cleared out the bathroom for her, and thus she was able to shower with plenty of hot water and use her pick of any of the uncloseted toilets in solitude.

"One hundred!" She sat up and wiped the sweat off her forehead. Her black, Western-style dress clung to her body. She rubbed the pleasurable ache in her left shoulder. Then she reversed her body, took three deep breaths, and recommenced her strange routine. "One, two, three . . ."

She had tried running in place once, but the unvarnished and uneven floor proved to be a torture to her bare feet (they had taken away her shoes), and when she stepped on a nail that was sticking up, invisible to her in the dark, she was fortunate that it only grazed the fleshy outstep.

She stared up at the block of light on the wall opposite the door. Normally she would see dark forms of people who were housed in the outer room passing by, but at the moment the square was undisturbed. They were out in the exercise yard between the barracks and the infirmary, enjoying the sun and sea air. Involuntarily she quickened her pace, flailing her arm wildly and kicking her feet.

Fatigue forced her to slow down and thus regain her form. Missing along with the usual shadows was the din that poured

Yoji Yamaguchi

in through the door—wailing children, scolding mothers, women fighting over territory in the small overcrowded room crammed wall to wall and up to the rafters with bunk beds. In this respect, her confinement was not so terrible: at least she did not live in that crammed squalor outside. "Twenty-three, twenty-four, twenty-five . . ."

Moreover, with her door padlocked at all hours, she was safe from the *hakujin* convicts who were housed at the other end of the floor. Hana remembered the day she cut her foot, when the matron escorted her to the clinic, past the prisoners' room: the leering white faces crowding in the doorway, the hooting and jeering in their foreign tongue, unintelligible yet unmistakable in tenor.

She dipped her hand too low, jamming her fingertips hard into the floor. Pain shot up her arm, and she cried out. The spell of exercise was broken, so she held her right hand to the light, to see if any of her nails were cracked or bleeding.

Better to be outside and take my chances with criminals, she thought. The cell was no more bearable than the stinking hold on the steamship in which she had been stowed away.

And all I did was ask for a private room, she thought as she lay on her back. But she knew that was not all. She should have known right away that she was bound for trouble, back in the port at Kobe.

There the agent of the labor contractor had led her down to the cargo hold of the ship and pointed to a narrow space, no more than four feet wide, behind a wall of crates and luggage. The agent, a mousy fellow with slicked-back hair by the name of Kumagai, relieved her of her suitcase and beckoned her to sit.

"Why?" she asked.

"It's for your protection. The American sailors are animals, barbarians; they especially like to prey on Japanese women. And when they're done with you, they'll throw you overboard. You must remain out of sight. Don't worry; once the ship is under way, someone will move you into more comfortable quarters."

For all his warnings about the Americans, it was a green-eyed, red-haired American sailor (bribed by Kumagai) who took care of her, sneaking her scraps from the mess and changing her slop bucket at every opportunity. He never spoke to her, and if he had any lewd designs, they were not terribly urgent; in fact, he rarely bothered to even look at her. Hana would have inquired why she had to hide among crates like so much contraband, but her English was too poor to ask.

Hana sat with her back against the wall and drew her knees up to her chest. In that tiny closet, she wondered for the first time whether running away from home might have been a mistake.

Her father, Nobuyuki Kuruzaki, was a labor recruiter for the Toyo Boseki plant in Osaka, part of one of the great manufacturing conglomerates spawned by the Meiji government's sale of state-owned factories and mills back in the 1870s. Nobuyuki made a more than comfortable living (a salary plus commission) traveling from town to town to hire women to work the cotton-spinning machines. The last of a struggling, undistin-

Yoji Yamaguchi

guished samurai family that had lost everything in the Restoration, he had formerly worked as a low-level clerk in the municipal office. Before Hana was born, he and his wife lived in a tiny, three-room house, which was all he could afford on his salary and his share of his late father's meager pension.

His fortunes turned dramatically when he chanced to run into an old middle school classmate while running an errand. No sooner had they exchanged pleasantries when the fellow, whom it must be said Nobuyuki never liked, began crowing about his family's purchase of five large cotton-spinning plants from the government for less than cost, adding with a wink that he understood finally why his father had bought so many expensive gifts for men he hardly knew. So pleased with himself was he—and no doubt noticing Nobuyuki's mean attire—that he magnanimously offered him a job on the spot. "You were always the charmer," his friend said, though Nobuyuki could not recall ever exchanging more than five words with the fellow. He considered telling him what he thought of him and his corrupt family for maybe half a minute before gratefully accepting.

A job was a job, after all; and it must be noted that Nobuyuki's compromise was largely motivated by concern for his then-pregnant wife and unborn child. In fact, one may attribute Hana's decidedly spoiled early upbringing to her father's distaste for both his employers and his job. The more he dwelled on his livelihood, the more he showered favors and gifts upon his child, as if to make amends for what he did during the day.

He also hired a full-time nanny—a needless extravagance,

by his wife's reckoning, and, as it turned out, one fraught with unforeseen consequences.

The nanny, a woman by the name of Také, was a spinster, heavyset, and in her middle age, with a rough-hewn face that could not be considered attractive. It was rumored that she had been engaged once, when she was twenty-two, only to have the wedding canceled at the last minute by her groom-to-be, who ran off with a teenage barmaid of striking good looks and decidedly easy virtue.

Disconsolate, the story went, Také gave up any hope of marriage and briefly flirted with the idea of shaving her head and becoming a nun. But after three or four occasions on which she was called upon to care for the children of her two younger sisters, she discovered that she had both an aptitude and an affinity for child rearing, and so hired herself out as a nanny instead.

Upon joining the Kuruzaki family's household, Také heard time and again Nobuyuki crow about his good luck. Hearing of the coincidence between the girl's birth and the rise in the family's fortunes, she was reminded of the fairy tale of the poor farmer who discovers a tiny baby inside a bamboo shoot that has turned to gold. One can only imagine the unhappy woman's state of mind as she went about her mischief.

"The baby was so small it fit in the palm of his hand," she would tell Hana at bedtime. "He brought her home to his wife and, because they were old and childless, they were very happy, and cared for her as if she were their own."

Hana lay down on her side on the rude wooden bench and

Yoji Yamaguchi

curled up with her knees against her chest. The sound of Také's low, throaty voice seemed to fill the dark cell.

"In three months she was of normal size, and quickly grew to be a most beautiful child.

"The farmer kept on harvesting his bamboo patch and kept on finding gold inside the shoots. In no time at all he became the richest man in the land. He built a huge mansion, hired hundreds of servants, and loaded his storehouse with treasures from around the world.

"But his wealth didn't spoil him or his wife, and they treated their adopted daughter with kindness, love, and gratitude.

"When she came of age, she was renowned throughout the land for her beauty. Soon an army of suitors swarmed down on the mansion. Lords of the highest rank showered her with love letters and expensive gifts.

"But she would have nothing to do with any of them. Those lucky enough to hear back from her were baffled by her strange replies. 'I want thunder from the sky,' she wrote one. 'Find a drum that beats itself,' she bade another. 'Bring me a flower from heaven,' she commanded a third. And so on.

"The lords, though all of them haughty and vain, tripped over themselves to oblige her. They traveled far and wide, asking priests and shamans how they might accomplish their impossible tasks. Some wandered the coasts, others through the mountains, only to lose their minds, or die homeless vagabonds.

"Finally, the emperor heard of the woman and her unlucky suitors and decided to take her for himself. He visited the old

111

couple's mansion with his train and met her face-to-face. Like the others, he fell madly in love with her.

" 'Come back with me to my palace,' he said. 'You'll be my empress.'

" 'I'd be happy to,' she said, 'but I can't. I'm not of this world, you see.'

"The emperor thought she was mocking him. 'What madness is this? Are you a demon? Or a goddess?' he asked, insulted.

" 'Neither,' she said. 'But I have to go now.' Then, to the amazement of all present, a throng of beings descended from the sky and bore her away. The emperor was desolate, but there was nothing to be done. Not even he could follow her."

Také told her many stories, but it was this one, of the beautiful maiden not of this world, that Hana insisted on hearing most often. To her mind—which, like those of most children her age, would brook no mystery—the tale was incomplete. Where did the pretty lady go, she wanted to know, where no man—not even the emperor—could intrude?

Hana could hear the women and children returning from the exercise yard to the barracks, where they would remain until lunchtime. She craned her neck, hoping to hear the sounds of girls squealing and laughing, but there was little of that there. Everyone seemed to carry themselves in a sullen daze. She lay back down.

Soon Hana outgrew bedtime stories and forgot the beautiful maiden. She grew not only into a handsome young girl herself, but a strong and athletic one also—too much so, for her parents' liking. By the time she was eight, she was not only the fastest runner of any age in her all-girls school, but faster than any local boy her age as well. And while her parents could understand, and even tolerate, the occasional hair-pulling and kicking skirmishes between her and some of her classmates, they were mortified when other parents began complaining to them of Hana roundly beating and humiliating their sons.

"This is all your fault," Nobuyuki grumbled to his wife. "You've let her grow up wild and undisciplined."

"And what about you?" Mrs. Kuruzaki rejoined. "You're always away on business or drinking with your buddies. Anyway, don't blame me; it's that nanny's fault—the one *you* hired. I told you she was a mistake." To that Nobuyuki had no reply; he simply threw up his hands and stormed out of the room.

Though he secretly agreed with his wife, Nobuyuki did not fire Také—not so much out of compassion, but simply because he did not want to acknowledge his error; and besides, it was such a bother. In any case, his wife took on the job of raising their daughter herself.

Hoping against hope to instill an iota of feminine refinement in her daughter before it was too late, Mrs. Kuruzaki sent Hana into a whirlwind of private lessons—music lessons, tea lessons, flower arranging, brush writing, etc.—but alas, to no avail. The young girl still bellowed when angry, guffawed when amused, spoke the blunt truth to anyone, and made unseemly, transparent faces; she wolfed down three helpings at every meal, and stomped heel-to-toe through their house, swinging her shoulders like a drill sergeant on parade.

Face of a Stranger

Then Mrs. Kuruzaki began receiving puzzling reports that her daughter had been absent from her lessons—puzzling, since Hana had been returning home at her usual hour. She began watching Hana arrive at the house and noted that on fair days as well as foul, her hair was invariably wet and her clothes damp. Mystified, she dispatched one of the maids to follow Hana from school and observe her from a distance.

The answer to the mystery almost caused Mrs. Kuruzaki to swoon: Hana had been spending her afternoons swimming alone, naked, in the inlet on the other side of town.

"Do many people swim there?" Mrs. Kuruzaki asked the maid, distraught.

The maid shook her head. "Nobody swims there; it's too dangerous. People say it's full of sharks! And that if they don't get you, the undertow will!" she squealed hysterically.

But Mrs. Kuruzaki was partly relieved: at least Hana was by herself. The last thing she wanted was some lecherous fisherman getting an eyeful of her daughter's young body.

Even that fact proved to be small comfort, though, when Mrs. Kuruzaki tried to rebuke Hana sternly for her conduct and was nearly floored by her daughter's reply: "Why not? I see boys swimming naked in the river all the time. Why can't I?"

What pained Mrs. Kuruzaki all the more was the girl's beauty, which grew more luminous with each passing year. By the time Hana was twelve, Mrs. Kuruzaki was certain she could marry her daughter off to any man she chose—if only she could restrain her from swimming naked, climbing trees, shouting and belching, terrorizing the help, or wrestling with boys.

Mrs. Kuruzaki was already at the point of despair when Hana came home from school one day reciting lines from a translation of an English play her class had been reading. "*Amadera ni makase*," she intoned.

"If thou dost marry, I'll give thee this plague for thy dowry: be thou chaste as ice, as pure as snow, thou shalt not escape calumny. *Amadera ni makase*. Go, farewell. Or if thou wilt need marry, marry a fool, for wise men know well enough what monsters you make of them. To a nunnery, go, and quickly too. *Abayo*."

For a month thereafter, whenever she was cross Hana would point her finger at her offender and shout "*Amadera ni makase*" in an imperious—and, to some ears, deranged—voice.

Mrs. Kuruzaki became increasingly concerned, and her fears were hardly assuaged when she procured a copy of the strange English play that had left such an impression. She read of the mad maiden's scandalous death by water with dread. To compound her distress, she learned that Hana continued to swim in the inlet despite her strict injunction.

"You call this discipline?" Nobuyuki hectored his wife. "You take over for Také and now the girl thinks she's a pearl diver or something."

Mrs. Kuruzaki decided to take no chances. She hired three burly women away from her husband's factory as lifeguards. Unlike the maid, who had espied Hana from behind a dune, these women stood on the jetty like statues, watching Hana cavort in the water. In time, at the girl's good-natured cajoling, they were stripping down themselves and joining her.

The precaution was unnecessary, as Hana was hardly inclined to drown herself, and the dangers of the inlet were largely a myth. Hana had become so adept that the older women, though stronger than her, could not keep up. In the water, she was not ungainly, flat-footed, or loud, but a picture of grace, native and apt in that element.

When she was fourteen, just as her parents had resigned themselves to her swimming habit, Hana greeted them with yet another shock. One morning a maid walked into her bedroom and screamed: the beautiful girl was taking her father's razor to her lustrous hair. The entire household was alerted and, after a tense and perilous struggle, Hana was relieved of the blade—though not before the damage was done: she had shorn the hair on the left side of her head up to her ear. While her mother wailed at the sight of her, Hana calmly announced her intention of becoming a nun.

"Are you still reading that damn play?" her father grumbled.

As half her hair was already chopped, her parents had no choice but to let her cut the rest. Mrs. Kuruzaki wrote a letter to the school to excuse her indefinitely, and kept her quarantined until her hair grew back to an acceptable length.

It was a difficult time for the entire household. Hana began to recite prayers and sutras, incomprehensible to her, from dawn to dusk until her throat was raw. She ate nothing but two mouthfuls of rice a day, and refused to drink anything but water, and even that sparingly. She gave up baths for ice-cold water ablutions, and wore the same dingy white kimono for an entire month.

"All day long, all she does is pray," Nobuyuki complained in the cups one night with a co-worker. Hana's rituals were forcing him to avoid the house as much as possible. "If I hear the Lotus Sutra one more time, I'll pull my hair out," he said.

"Eh, then you could be a priest yourself—a real 'shaved head'!" his colleague cackled, but Nobuyuki was not amused.

To her parents' relief, after three months or so of prayers, cold baths, and fasting, Hana gave up the holy life. Her regimen seemed to have had little effect on her, save a pair of aching knees, a nagging flu, and a ravenous hunger.

By then her hair had grown back to more or less normal length, and with timid hope Mrs. Kuruzaki allowed her to return to school. She hired three more women from the factory, doubling Hana's bodyguard. The six women followed her everywhere, even into the classroom, much to the amusement of Hana's classmates.

To Mrs. Kuruzaki's surprise, Hana forsook her daily trips to the inlet to stay after school in order to catch up. The principal reported proudly that Hana was being personally tutored by the school's newest teacher, a brilliant young woman come all the way from Tokyo.

At last Mrs. Kuruzaki began to feel that her beautiful daughter would grow up normal after all. But her complacency was short-lived. By the time of Hana's fifteenth birthday, Mrs. Kuruzaki was already fretting at the apparent lack of interest in her daughter among the families of eligible young men.

"She's the prettiest girl in town and no one seems to notice her," she lamented one night.

"Of course not," her husband cracked. "She's beaten up every boy at least once. Who wants a wife like that? What a fine monkey you've raised her to be!" Mrs. Kuruzaki stormed out of the room.

One day one of the maids anxiously presented Mrs. Kuruzaki with a dog-eared copy of a magazine she had found in Hana's closet. It bore the unlikely name of *Bluestockings*.

Mrs. Kuruzaki flipped through it quickly, perusing the articles. What she saw shocked her: "Men and Women Are Equals," "The New Woman," "The Liberation of the New Woman." There was also poetry, the likes of which she had never seen before:

> All the sleeping women
> Are now awake and moving.

"What kind of nonsense is this for a young girl to be reading?" Nobuyuki growled after his wife showed him the magazine.

"Where could it have come from?" Mrs. Kuruzaki wondered.

They stared at each other for but a second when it occurred to them: the new teacher.

With distaste, Nobuyuki called on his old classmate once again for help. He asked him to use his contacts in Tokyo to investigate both the scurrilous publication and the young teacher.

The answers to his questions about *Bluestockings* were not long in coming; in fact, he hardly needed the help of a professional investigator, as the magazine had become quite a sensation up in Tokyo (a fact that, when pointed out to him by his classmate, made him feel provincial). The detective sent him a dossier full of newspaper clippings about the magazine and its publishers, one of which nearly caused Mrs. Kuruzaki to swoon:

SEITŌ NEW WOMEN, SEEKING EQUAL RIGHTS WITH MEN, SPEND NIGHT OF PLEASURE WITH YOSHIWARA PROSTITUTE.

Against her will, Mrs. Kuruzaki listened as Nobuyuki read the detective's official report: *Bluestockings* (Seitō) was a literary magazine propagating all kinds of wild stuff and nonsense about the so-called new women—who believed themselves equal to men and that they should be treated as such, and displayed utter disregard and disrespect for basic values about family, marriage, society, and even the emperor. The more radical elements of the Seitō group were suspected to be Communists. The leader of the group and the magazine's founder was a woman named Hiratsuka, an unmarried woman of questionable morals, said to have a fondness for five-colored liqueurs and young men half her age.

The teacher in question, the report went on, was a minor member of the group. She was formerly employed by a primary school in Tokyo but was forced to resign in disgrace when her affiliation with Seitō became known. (There were unconfirmed stories, the report noted, of an amorous affair between her and the husband of another member—a much older man, whose once-promising career as a man of letters was thwarted by drink and debauchery.)

"Ah ha!" Nobuyuki cried out triumphantly. "I bet she was the one who made Hana read that stupid play. Don't worry, I'll fix everything," he boasted. Mrs. Kuruzaki was not so sure, but knew there would be no reasoning with him.

The next day after work Nobuyuki visited the school principal at his home and revealed the teacher's sordid past. Invoking his family's name (which, alas, drew a blank with the fellow), Nobuyuki loudly demanded the teacher's termination, on pain of his daughter's immediate withdrawal from school and any scandal that might ensue. The principal, in truth wishing for the former possibility but dreading the latter, quickly acquiesced. As an afterthought, Nobuyuki demanded that the Englishman's play *Hamuretto* be removed from the school's curriculum; the principal agreed to that as well, mainly to get him out of his house, but never carried out the promise.

Though Hana appeared quite unmoved at the news of her teacher's departure (for "reasons of health," the principal had announced), Nobuyuki was quite proud of the way he handled the matter, much to his wife's annoyance. A month later, however, Mrs. Kuruzaki greeted her husband from work with more bad news: "Hana wants to get a job—a laborer's job." Scarcely able to conceal her glee, she jeered at her husband. "I thought you were going to fix everything! You call this discipline? Now she wants to be a field hand or something! What a fine monkey you've raised her to be!"

Yoji Yamaguchi

Nobuyuki was apoplectic. "A job? Outrageous! Out of the question! I didn't raise my daughter to be a factory girl!" As soon as those words left his lips, he was struck with yet another brilliant idea. "Don't you worry: this time I'll *really* fix everything!" Mrs. Kuruzaki walked out of the room, laughing to herself.

The next day Nobuyuki caused quite a stir at the factory by bringing his daughter. He wanted to show her the wretched conditions in which the women workers had to live and work, and thus rid her of her latest whim.

One must appreciate the difficulty of Nobuyuki's position: whereas his job normally entailed gulling women into working in barbarous conditions with just the right mix of honeyed words, gloss, exaggeration, and outright lies, Nobuyuki found himself trying to impress upon his own daughter the squalor and the degradation of life in the factory—in short, for a change he had to tell the truth.

Yet he was nothing if not persuasive. Besides, the ugliness of factory life was readily apparent to anyone with eyes to see—or so he thought.

"See this tiny room?" he whispered, opening a door to a darkened room not much bigger than her own. "Twenty women sharing ten mattresses. The women sleeping here now work on the night shift. When they go to work, the women from the day shift take their place."

"And look at this bath," he said later. "The water is changed maybe once a week. Look how cloudy it is; the women say it sticks to your skin after you get out."

121

He took her onto the plant floor. "Look at the machines, how big they are! Each woman runs a machine all by herself. Noisy, aren't they? Really hurt the ears. They never shut down, not even a minute, unless they get fouled or break down, and if that happens, the operator loses a full day's wage. Look: everybody has to stand; there are no chairs for sitting. No, on your feet for the full twelve hours—we don't want our workers to get too comfortable. Oh, there's a bathroom upstairs, but most women won't use it until the end of their shifts, because it's too much time away from their machines."

At lunchtime he took her to the mess hall and they sat down at one of the long tables with the workers. "Listen to these women talking: what gibberish! They're mostly from the country, and quite a few are Okinawans. It's like a barn in here! I can't imagine spending a whole day with them."

He examined his tray. "Whew! Cabbage again! That's the third time they've served it this week. I bet it's been cooked a dozen times! And this rice! It looks like glue! Oh well, it can't be helped, I guess. Come on, eat up; you'll need your strength. I've got lots more to show you."

Nobuyuki might have accomplished his goal had it not been for an untimely and, as it turned out, disastrous interruption. As the two were picking at their respective trays of slop, one of his underlings, a fellow by the name of Takeshita, bustled to their table to whisper a message in his ear.

One of the workers, who owed the company thirty yen from her advance, had tried to make a run for it, he reported. She got as far as the train station when the local police, whose chief duty seemed to be tracking down wayward employees from the factory, apprehended her. She was being held at the police box on Jūsan-chome.

Now there was a dilemma. Returning escapees to the factory was a humiliating chore, as they invariably took him to task for their distress, usually in a most scandalous fashion. He did not want his daughter to witness him being dressed down by a laborer, and a woman at that; on the other hand, he could not very well leave her to her own devices. He decided, finally, to leave her in the care of Takeshita.

Though eight years Hana's senior, Takeshita could not help staring at the boss's beautiful daughter, whose looks far exceeded her years. Sitting beside her, he tried mightily to put up an aloof, indifferent air, but after a minute or so he was reduced to a sweating, trembling wreck. By contrast, Hana seemed scarcely aware of his presence.

The women sitting around the unlikely couple did not help matters with their giggling and carrying on; he blushed an angry red and stumbled up from the table. Furious at the women, and at his boss for putting him in such a shameful predicament, Takeshita began to pace up and down the rows of tables with his hands behind his back, as if he were a supervisor.

As soon as Takeshita left the table, two women sidled up to Hana and sat down on each side of her. One, who was not much older than Hana, leaned over and hissed: "So, the snake's found himself another bird?"

Hana did not reply but simply picked at her unappetizing fare. The other woman, who was closer to Hana's parents in age, chided her companion: "Don't talk like that to her; she's just a kid." Then she spoke to Hana: "You're Kuruzaki's daughter, aren't you."

Hana nodded. "Why'd you come here?" the younger woman challenged. "You come to laugh at us or something?" Hana said nothing.

"You didn't come here to work, did you?" the older woman asked. "He didn't bring you here to work, did he?"

"Oh excellent!" the younger woman sneered. "He'll even sell his own girl to these pigs—and probably pocket a fat commission for himself, too!" She laughed venomously. "Hmmm—such a pretty thing, too," she said. "What's the matter—some guy break your heart or something?" She put her arm around Hana and squeezed her shoulder. "I'd never do that," she said.

Her companion slapped her hand away from Hana. "Enough of your jokes!" The younger woman shrugged and turned back to her food.

The older woman gave Hana a thoughtful look. "Listen to me," she said. "Everything your father's told you about this place is a lie. You hear me? I know he's your father and I can tell he takes good care of you—such fancy clothes, neh!—but he's a liar. That's his job. He's lied to everyone in this room—including you."

But Hana was not listening. She was looking around the mess hall; it was packed entirely with women—of all ages, all dressed in the same drab gray, their heads covered with white kerchiefs. She observed them laughing, cursing, exchanging elbows and sly glances. Her father was right: their dialects, their vernacular, were unfamiliar to her. And yet, she could fathom what they were saying, by the sounds of their voices, the looks in their faces.

"Hey, are you listening?" the older woman nudged her. "Remember what I said: don't believe him, don't let him talk you into anything."

"He's her father," the younger woman said. "What's she going to do? Run away from home? Maybe she can go to America and get rich!" She laughed.

The older woman glared at her, then turned to Hana. "Just remember what I said." A horn sounded, and when Hana looked up, the two women were already gone.

Nobuyuki returned an hour later in a peevish mood; as he had expected, the woman insulted him roundly—in front of two patrolmen, no less. He dismissed his underling, announcing that he was taking his daughter home.

Hana was not sure when she had made up her mind to leave him and her mother, or exactly what persuaded her. Maybe it was the speech her father gave her on their way home from the factory.

"What a terrible place it is," he clucked, shaking his head. "Awful conditions, grueling work, trashy women . . . brrrrr!" He shuddered. "But I feel sorry for them, I do. None of them will ever get married; they'll become old maids, working till they die. They have a tough lot, they do.

"But you're not like them: they have no schooling, no prospects; most of them are lucky to have their jobs. But you—that's no kind of life for you. You don't want to end up haggard and worn out in five years, do you? Iya; better to get a husband and let him do all the work, while you stay in a nice house like ours, raising beautiful children."

She snuck out of their home three months later, with a suitcase and whatever money she was able to scrape together. The woman who called herself Oshichi found her at the train station and quickly took her under her wing. Hana almost laughed when the old woman gave her pitch, which sounded nearly identical to her father's—challenging work, good pay, generous bonus, educational opportunities, room and board—the only difference, a crucial one, being the promise of America. "A woman can be anything she wants to be over there," the clever crone wheezed.

Hana had a good idea what the woman was about, she knew now, and yet it did not matter to her at the time. Or perhaps it did, she reflected: perhaps it could not have been otherwise.

She stood up to stretch her legs and yawned loudly. She could hear the heavyset barracks matron approaching her cell, a ring of keys dangling, jangling from her hand.

Yoji Yamaguchi

Kikue paced the diameter of her room at the Pacific Hotel. It was three days since she had left Arai passed out on her bed and returned the next morning to find him gone. She had expected him to come back, and when he failed to appear the next night, and the two nights after that, Kikue felt, oddly enough, a little scorned. She was sorely tempted to search him out, but knew she could not without the risk of making him suspicious.

He had wanted her once more. What did it mean? she wondered. Why her? She had never attracted anyone but boys and old men before she started her moneylending business. From the looks of Arai, she would have assumed him too vain to consort with a woman who was not at least as beautiful as him. And yet he came back, conscious and sober, with money in his hand.

Of course, he did not look well. He was pale and sweating, shivering uncontrollably, she recalled. No doubt he had a fever, and was probably delirious. He really didn't know what he was doing.

And what of her? Why her confusion, her alarm, when he proffered the money and smiled? Was he not just another *buranke katsugi*, a migrant worker with patched-up clothes and no place to call home? Why her dread at the thought of his touch, his body on hers? Hadn't she done enough men so that she no longer felt anything? Why would he be any different?

Because of him you were robbed of your past and future, left only with a present that is a lie, just as he is a lie, an illusion made flesh; inside you, he would fill you with his very falseness, and it would obliterate, negate you, so that you would be nobody, nothing, an illusion just like him, just like the thing Kato would have you become.

Nonsense, she thought, chiding herself for her sentimentality. There was only one thing she wanted from Arai: his comeuppance. As if to resolve herself to that end, she rehearsed in her mind the story she would tell Arai to propose the phony marriage: that Hana Kuruzaki is the only daughter of a rich family looking for a son-in-law to adopt as male heir. Hana's beauty together with the promise of a dowry of unimaginable riches should be enough, she convinced herself, to gull the transparently stupid Arai.

But just when it looked as if her plan was in motion, Arai had to disappear, Kikue thought peevishly. She decided to see Shino, even though it was the middle of the day and her friend

Yoji Yamaguchi

was probably asleep. Shino had a way of finding out anything, Kikue assured herself.

She dressed before the full-length mirror: a severe brown skirt and waistcoat, a white blouse with a high, stiff collar, and a wide-brimmed hat topped with downy plumage. The only other time she had worn these clothes was when she moved into the hotel, a concession she made to nervous Inada. Kikue decided to dress in the Western fashion after Shino's run-in with Mrs. Inada two days before.

Kikue had not failed to notice that the woman had since been even colder toward her than usual, which was hardly surprising; but she also noticed that Inada himself was more brusque toward her, not his usual diffident self. She wondered if anything was afoot, but she was too preoccupied with Arai to give Inada much thought. Arai's absence seemed to make her even more determined to teach him a lesson.

She left the hotel without incident and arrived at Shino's hut without anyone noticing her finery. Shino was awake when she arrived. As soon as Kikue set foot inside the hut, her friend burst out laughing.

"You should see yourself. What are you—a mission lady?" Shino chortled. "You've been living in that hotel too long, I think. Take care—pretty soon you might end up looking like that warthog who runs the place."

Kikue frowned. Shino could be annoying sometimes.

Yet she was nothing if not perceptive. When she saw Kikue's expression, she stopped laughing; her face at once turned solemn. "So," she said. "Do you know what happened to Arai?"

"No," Kikue hissed, more anxious than she had realized. "Do you?"

"I don't guess you'll be seeing him anytime soon."

"Why? Is he in trouble?"

"He's out of a job. I heard it from the boy who replaced him, a kid named Ishikawa; he was here last night." A furtive smile crossed her face. "I think it was his first time."

"So what happened to Arai?" Kikue asked impatiently.

"Seems he was working for two old hakujin. They fired him on the spot when he showed up late for work."

"So what did he do? Where did he go? Did he leave town?"

"Probably not. His bosses didn't pay him for his last two days. If the money you took off him the other night was all he had, then he's flat broke."

"But where did he go?"

"I don't know, but I'll bet Nakagami has seen him in the past few days."

A pained look crossed Kikue's face. She crossed her arms and stared pensively at the floor.

"Neh, why so glum?" Shino asked. "This is perfect."

"Why?"

"Now Arai is not only broke, he's out of a job. I've been asking around about him. Seems he can't hold down a job for more than six months. He's a terrible gambler, an even worse pool player, so he's always losing money. He's ripe to be picked. So if you tell him that the girl is an only child to rich parents and that a marriage to her would set him up for life, I'll bet you wouldn't even have to show him her picture—though if you do

130

Yoji Yamaguchi

he'll be sure to go along. A beautiful girl with a fortune to give: what more could a bum like him want?"

Kikue reflected on Shino's argument: as always, she made perfect sense. "I guess you're right. Now if only we knew where he is."

"So go to Nakagami's bar. If you're lucky, he'll be there, drunk and feeling sorry for himself; you could probably convince him to marry that bitch Inada then. Hurry, go!" Shino waved her arms imperiously. Kikue laughed and bowed like a maid, and hustled out.

She hurried down the alley, ignoring the sounds of the women at work in their huts. Something to her left caught her eye. She turned and cried out in alarm. Leaning against the doorway of one of the huts was what looked like a skeleton. It was Wada, the senior of Kato's prostitutes. Her bloodshot eyes were puffy, nearly shut, and she wore a lascivious grin. With her bony hand she beckoned.

Kikue could smell the cloying fumes of opium wafting from the open door. She shuddered and broke into a run, anxious to get away. She could hear the woman's laughter, a dry, rasping cackle, behind her.

As she approached the business district, the prospect began to brighten: shacks gave way to whitewashed, immaculate one-family residences, each with a neatly trimmed, if not quite fecund, lawn and an obligatory row of flowers or shrubbery. Soon she was on J Street, and as she came up to Nakagami's saloon, she saw the door open, and a young boy stick his head out; when he saw her, an alarmed look crossed his face, and he

131

quickly ducked back inside. She shrugged and proceeded leisurely to the saloon.

When she entered, Kikue thought she had walked into the wrong place. The usually seedy bar looked like a middle school playroom. Each table was adorned with a red-and-white-checkered tablecloth and a small flower arrangement. On the far wall hung a portrait of the American president, bracketed by the American and Japanese flags respectively. At one table, two men were intently studying a chessboard; next to them, another man was sitting alone, sipping tea and reading a translation of Lafcadio Hearn. The rest were quietly discussing events of the day with a studied gravity. There was not a drink to be seen anywhere; as if to emphasize that lack, Nakagami called out from behind the bar, "Would anyone care for more tea?" and with a flourish held up a pot.

Nonplussed, Kikue approached the bar. "Nakagami," she whispered, "what's going on here?"

Nakagami, a stout, square-faced man in his forties, frowned at her, puzzled; then he broke into a smile of surprise and relief. "Ah, it's you. We thought you were one of those women from the church." He announced to the room: "Hey boys! It's all right—the show's over," then glared darkly at the boy she had seen at the door, who was now busy collecting teacups. "Masuji!" Nakagami barked.

The skinny boy ran to the bar, struggling to balance a loaded tray. "Hai."

"What's the matter with you? How could you mistake Kikue here for a mission lady?"

Masuji, a sixteen-year-old who looked more like twelve, bowed jerkily, nearly upsetting his tray in the process. "Gomen nasai. I didn't recognize you. I mean . . . you're not dressed like a whore today."

"Damare! Bakayaro! Get out of here!" Nakagami shouted, rearing back to cuff the boy, who fled in a panic. He had good reason to rage at Masuji, as Kikue held a fifty percent interest in his saloon. "Please forgive me," Nakagami apologized solemnly. "He's just young and stupid."

Kikue surveyed the bar: the tablecloths, flowers, banner, flags, and American president were gone, as were all the teacups, replaced by glasses and bottles of whiskey. The conversation grew loud and animated, except for the two chess players, who had apparently missed the cue. "So what was that all about?" she asked.

Nakagami shook his head. "Ehh to—those mission ladies are trying to run me out of business. They come in here now and then to give me a hard time, tell me I'm ruining the morals of the dekaseginin and disgracing our country. Then they start pestering the customers, recruiting them for their church. Urusai da yo! So whenever they come by we put on this show, and usually they just leave in a huff. I guess it's no good for them unless they catch us off guard.

"It's getting worse, though. Now the consulate is getting into the act. Oh, they don't give a damn about our morals; they're only worried about appearances. They don't like it when we have a good time in public. Twice they asked me to move my place into a back room, like a secret club. What the hell, I told them, business is too good as it is—what with all the blanket carriers between jobs—so forget it. So I put up those flags to keep the consulate guys happy."

Behind her Kikue could hear the two chess players still debating: "Ah, tha's true, but remember what Fukuzawa wrote in *Seiyo Jijo* . . ."

"Hey, knock it off, I said!" Nakagami bellowed. "It was only a false alarm."

One of the men rose deliberately, albeit unsteadily, from his chair, and stood up stiffly. He intoned slowly: "We were havin' a . . . conversation . . . you know."

"Ah *shitsurei shimashita,*" Nakagami apologized with mock humility, bowing low. The man sniffed in disdain and plopped back in his chair to resume his exposition.

"Nakagami," Kikue said in a low voice, leaning slightly over the bar.

"Hmmm?"

"Has Arai been here lately?"

Nakagami's face darkened. "Master Face? That piece of shit? Yeah, he was here. Tried to stiff me for a tab. Damn near kicked his worthless ass!"

"Do you know where he went?"

"He left with that imo Doi."

"Doi Kogoro?"

"Umm. Good thing for Arai he showed up, too. I caught that namakemono at the door, trying to sneak out. Gave me a sob story about how he just lost all his money and had no job. Well, I said, you shouldn't be drinking my whiskey then! I was about to bust his face when Doi walked in." Nakagami spat. "Arai started begging the guy for help, so Doi just emptied his pockets and paid off his tab. Can you believe that?"

"So then what happened?" Kikue asked.

"Well, since Doi was so easy with his money, Arai decided he needed a few more for the road. He made Doi listen to his story all over again. So Doi invited him to stay at his farm and work for him until he found a new job and place to live. Baka na!"

"Arai went to Doi's farm?"

"Yeah. As if Doi needs any help; he could work half the fields in California by himself! And besides, if he really wanted good help, there are a dozen men in this room who'd be better for the job than that guy. I don't know; maybe they had something else on their minds." Nakagami gave her a sly smile.

Before Kikue could respond, both were distracted by shouting and a loud crash. They turned to see the two old scholars throttling one another, their table lying on its side between them. One of the men was dripping with beer. The men in the bar circled round them, cheering them on.

"Oi! Oi! No fighting!" Nakagami roared. With surprising agility, he leapt between the two and separated them, sending both men flying onto their backs.

"What is this shit?" he barked, glowering down at them both, hands on his hips. The two men rose painfully to their feet. "You geezers fighting over a woman? Eh?" Laughter erupted from the crowd.

The old man who had spoken to him before said in a tremu-

Face of a Stranger

lous voice: "We were arguing over the merits of *naimenteki na dōka*."

"'Internal assimilation'? What the hell is that?"

"The idea that we should not only act like Americans, but think like them as well."

"And for that you're going to wreck my bar? Get out of here!" Another roar of laughter filled the room.

Kikue was scarcely aware of what was happening; her mind was on what to do about Arai. Silently she beckoned the boy Masuji, who approached her with trepidation.

"Tell Nakagami to arrange a ride for me tomorrow."

"H-hai," he replied, nodding vigorously. As she turned to leave, he blurted out: "Wait."

She whirled around. "What?"

"Uh . . . where you going?"

Kikue scrutinized the boy a long time, as if trying to decide something, much to Masuji's discomfort. Finally, she told him simply: "Doi's farm. I'm going to see Doi Kogoro."

Then she slipped quietly out of the bar as the debate over the Americanization of the Issei raged on.

When Inada was summoned by Kikue to her room, he was not at all prepared for what she had to tell him. "Please excuse my friend the other day. I hope she did not upset you and your wife too much."

Inada could only stammer: "Oh, no, no. . . ." He wondered whence came this sudden fit of humility on Kikue's part.

"She's a country girl, you see," she continued. "The people

who brought her here, our employers, did not have time to teach her the proper etiquette." Inada did not fail to notice the edge in her voice. So much for humility. "I hope your other guests were not disturbed by all the fuss."

Inada thought of randy Tsushida, lust burning through the rheum in his old eyes, and blushed. "Er, not at all."

"I can assure you it won't happen again," Kikue said.

"Thank you."

They were both startled by the sound of Mrs. Inada's angry voice two floors below, mixed with what sounded like the frantic cries of a boy. Without a word, they both quit the room and bounded down the stairs. At the first landing, they were nearly overrun by three guests who were scrambling to their rooms. "What's wrong?" Inada asked, but they did not stop to answer.

Inada reached the lobby first, and looked into the dining room. He saw his wife jabbing a broom at a young boy who was cowering under the table, trying to flush him out.

"Ouch, ouch! Leave me alone! What'd I do?" the boy was crying.

"I won't have it! I won't have you lowlifes parading into our hotel to see that whore!" she railed. "And look at you! You're just a boy! You should be in school, not chasing after loose women! What would your mother say?"

"M-my m-mother's . . . dead," the boy stammered.

"Lucky for her she's not alive to see you now; may she rest in peace. What a burden, to have a good-for-nothing son!" She jabbed him again. He yelped as the broom head found its mark.

"Sumiko, what is this?" Inada asked.

As she turned to reply, the boy saw his chance, and sprang out from beneath the table, flopping at Inada's feet. "Help, sir, she's trying to kill me," he panted.

"On your feet!" she bellowed, kicking him in the seat of his pants. He leapt to his feet and scrambled around Inada, using him as a shield.

"He's come to see that whore," Sumiko said, her voice choked with disgust. "Look at him! Why, he's younger than Imoyaro, and already he's catting around! You wouldn't catch Imoyaro in a brothel!" she shouted at the boy.

"Who's that, your grandson?" the boy asked.

Her eyes widened, and she raised the broom over her head, ready to strike a terrible blow. Inada grabbed her arms. "No, no, that won't do," he said.

"Masuji! What are you doing here?" Kikue demanded.

The boy ran to her, stopped and bowed nervously. "Uh, Shino said you'd be here."

Kikue glanced quickly at the Inadas, who were busy grappling over the broom. "So, why did you come?"

"Uh, I was looking for you."

Kikue grimaced impatiently. "Why?"

"You said you wanted a ride to Doi's farm."

"Yes?"

"It's waiting for you at the bar."

Exasperated, she cuffed him on the head. "Why didn't you say so in the first place?"

"Nan da yo!" the boy whined, rubbing his scalp. "Everybody's hitting me today."

Yoji Yamaguchi

"Stop crying," she said. "Take me there."

Though Inada had wrested the broom away from his wife, Masuji sprinted past the couple, with Kikue scurrying to catch up. "Please excuse us," she said. Inada gave her a curt bow while his wife glared at her sullenly. He noticed that Sumiko always seemed to clam up whenever the prostitute was around; it was only in her absence that she berated her.

Inada was exhausted. He and his wife stared vacantly at the closed door. "For whoever causes one of these children to sin, there will be no forgiveness," she mumbled sadly. He stared at her, surprised at how quickly her rage had been deflated.

Then the door opened a crack, and Masuji's head appeared. "See ya, Grandma!" he piped and stuck out his tongue. Before they could react, he was gone.

Kikue was out of breath after chasing Masuji all the way to Nakagami's. When they walked into the saloon, Nakagami spotted Masuji right away and bellowed: "Oi! Where the hell you been?" He stalked toward them with his fists clenched and an angry gleam in his eye.

"Oh, no, not you, too!" Masuji wailed and covered his head with both hands. As Nakagami raised his arm to strike, Kikue held out her hand to stay him. "Chotto." Nakagami stared at her, perplexed, as if noticing her for the first time. Masuji peeked out through his elbows and relaxed.

Kikue turned to Masuji and asked: "Well, where's my ride?"

"Wait here," Masuji said and sidled over to an old man sitting at the bar. He whispered briefly in his ear. The man rose from his stool and walked crablike toward Kikue and Nakagami, with Masuji trailing behind. The old man bowed. "Hajimema-shite. I am Kimura. I would be pleased to take you wherever you wish to go," he said solemnly.

Kikue bowed as well. "Thank you for your trouble. May we go now?"

"Of course. Eh, allow me to bring my truck up to the door." Slowly he ambled out the door.

"Strange old bird," Nakagami said.

"Yes," Kikue replied. "Is he married?"

"Nah. Kinda sad, these old bachelors. Living by themselves, no wife, they can't even have any fun. They're too old to do anything with a woman; all they can do is think about it, try to remember what it was like. It must be a real torture," Nakagami said, a little wistfully. Kikue glanced at him, surprised.

A horn honked outside. "Ah, there's my ride," Kikue said and headed toward the door. "Thanks for your help."

"Not at all. See you later."

She climbed into the cab of the truck that stank of cigar smoke and motor oil. "Do you know where Doi lives?" she asked.

"Indeed," Kimura replied. They drove off slowly. The old man turned to Kikue and said, "Pardon me for saying, but you really are quite beautiful. You remind me of a girl I once knew, back in Sendai. . . ."

Oh great, Kikue thought, and stared out the window. She wondered how long the drive would be.

Yoji Yamaguchi

eight

When Kogoro found Takashi in Nakagami's saloon, raving at the bartender, he assumed that all his drunken friend needed to clear his head was a good night's sleep. But after two days on his farm, without a drop to drink (Kogoro, who never drank anything more than an occasional beer at Nakagami's, kept his home bone-dry), Takashi's behavior seemed even more bizarre. Kogoro assumed that his friend's shivering and sweating had something to do with his apparent madness. The few times Kogoro tried to speak to him he was left scratching his head.

"Arai-san . . . "

"Don't call me that. Call me Charlie."

"Uhn?"

"Charlie. *Chaa-rii.* That's my name now. Yours, too. We're both Charlies. *Pleased to meet you, Mistah Chaarii.*

141

Joozu, ne? Charlies hafta be fluent in English, y'know." Takashi thrust out his hand; Kogoro couldn't help flinching. "Nan da? Don't you know how to shake hands? That's what Charlies do; no bowing."

"I don't understand."

"Ah, wakaranai ka? You must learn English; I'll teach you. Kiite kure: *Guuud maawning, iss deesu Missus Sumisu hausu?* Jya, onegai shimasu." Kogoro could only gape at him. Takashi thew up his hands and scoffed: "Ah, forget it. Whew—where's the benjo? I gotta take a leak."

Seeing Takashi in such a state, Kogoro could not help but feel guilty for his friend's (there was no other word) failure and his own inexplicable success: inexplicable because when he arrived in America he knew little of farming—in fact, he knew little of anything. All he was good for, it seemed, was causing others heartache and vexation. He remembered his father's last tortured days, when all the sake he had drunk—on Kogoro's account, he knew—finally took its toll.

Despite his prodigious size as a young boy, Kogoro was subjected to all kinds of ridicule by his peers. His rough features, his abnormally guttural voice, and his utter lack of anger people took as signs of a feeble mind. His three older brothers, Ichiro, Jiro, and Saburo, who were hyperconscious of their social standing, as boys at that age usually are, shunned their freakish sibling. Whether they had been encouraged to do so by their father is uncertain, though it could hardly have been a coincidence that Kogoro's given name did not follow suit with those of brothers One, Two, and Three.

Yoji Yamaguchi

One day when he was eight, Kogoro was trailing behind five other boys on the beach. About twenty yards or so up ahead, he saw his three brothers standing on a dune, watching him and his mates approach. Then Ichiro began waving his arms, and one of the boys said, "Now," whereupon the whole group rushed Kogoro and gang-tackled him. They tried to drag him into the surf; he resisted. When it was over thirty seconds later, the five boys suffered between them one broken nose, two black eyes, three fractured ribs, four teeth lost, untold scrapes and bruises. Other than a badly rent shirt and a bucketful of sand in his britches, Kogoro was none the worse for wear. His brothers were nowhere in sight.

In the end, though, it was Kogoro who suffered most. News of his rampage on the beach quickly spread through the village of Kunioku. He was depicted as a crazed feral child run amok, growling and (some said) even foaming at the mouth as he attacked his schoolmates without provocation or warning. Children began fleeing in terror at the sight of him. His brothers would not sit in the same room with him; at night they each took turns standing watch, lest he massacre them in their sleep. A mob of frightened parents besieged the Doi home, demanding that Kogoro be sent away, far away, for good.

To his credit, Mr. Doi refused—though, it must be said, he was not acting out of paternal love; he simply refused to be blamed for Kogoro's actions. By his reckoning, he was the only real victim, having been cursed with a monstrosity of a son. Regrettably, his pride (and more than a few flasks of sake) got the better of him, and he began taunting the other parents, calling their children cowards and weaklings and dwarves. The crowd eventually dispersed, but the damage was done: the Doi family was ostracized by the village.

Because he was deemed a menace, Kogoro was remanded to the home, where he was given such domestic chores as cooking, sweeping, airing out the mats, washing and mending clothes, and tending the small garden out back. The local children, emboldened by his house arrest, ran past the Doi house, or else stood at a safe distance, and called him beached whale, fat girl, pussy, etc.

By the time Kogoro was sixteen or so, his father—who had earned local renown in his youth for his love of drink—could no longer work; his few sober hours he would spend curled up in bed, mumbling incoherently to himself. He stopped eating and lost thirty pounds from his already lean, wiry frame; his face sunk in, as if it had lost its bones, and his joints stuck out like knobs. Kogoro's mother tried to rouse her husband out of his decline by appealing to his sense of paternal duty. "A fine example you're setting for your sons! If you won't act like a man for your own sake, then at least do it for your children's," she railed one day. The last thing that Doi needed to hear was a lecture on parental duty as he watched Kogoro—the infernal curse upon his life—intent on one of his woman's chores, his eyebrows knitted and his tongue poking out like an idiot's.

When his body washed up on the beach two weeks later, Kunioku was abuzz with speculation on the nature of his death—suicide or accident? The villagers forgot their feud with the dead man and were duly solicitous toward his grieving widow and sons. Among themselves, however, they clucked, whispered, shook their heads, treating the whole scandal like some kind of morality play: Doi had always been a vain man, an arrogant man, they said; Kogoro, the humble, bumbling, ungainly oaf, was his punishment, his bane, his sufferance. No one said as much, but they all knew the real cause of Doi's untimely demise.

Everyone, that is, except the Doi boys. A month after their father's death, Kogoro's brothers—who would not even acknowledge his presence—were still lamenting among themselves, loud enough for him to hear, how the shame of such a worthless son was too much for their father, for anyone, to bear. More to the point, they wondered aloud, how would the family support itself? Perchance, Ichiro had heard of a labor contractor making the rounds in nearby Tsugaru, recruiting *dekaseginin* for a big American company. When Kogoro saw the shit-eating grins on their faces as they looked his way for the first time in weeks, he knew his days at home were numbered.

Not that Kogoro minded; if anything, he was eager to escape the oppressive guilt that hung over him in that place. No one blamed him for his father's death more than Kogoro himself. All too well he understood the twitch of disgust in his father's face whenever he deigned to look at his misfit son; or his long-winded sighs of disappointment punctuating the night like storm winds. Maybe in America, alone, free of expectations or obligations, he could somehow manage to avoid hurting anyone else.

How topsy-turvy everything was, Kogoro thought as he sat

on the stoop of his small farmhouse, staring at the road. He could not fathom why he should flourish while Takashi suffered so abjectly, when it was readily apparent to him that his friend was his superior, simply by dint of his elegant face, the assured manner in which he carried himself, his educated way of speaking. Kogoro could not help but think that Takashi's poverty was the result of his own prosperity; that he had somehow usurped the weal that was rightfully, deservedly, Takashi's, leaving Takashi in the misery that should have been his. Kogoro of course knew nothing of Takashi's ignoble past, his banishment from his father's house—or, more important, the heartache and vexation he had caused in his own right.

In the distance he could see a truck approaching in a small but thick cloud of dust. Though he never had many visitors at his farm, for some reason he knew that it was heading his way.

Takashi slept fitfully, his body seized by chills and his mind overrun by a river of images, one after another in rapid succession.

Aya, his nanny, is a stone-faced dumpling of indeterminate years; she has served Takashi's family for two generations seemingly without aging a day. Takashi's father once said that Aya was born (and would die) a surly middle-aged woman.

She is in the family kitchen, preparing treats for Takashi and his brother, Keichi. Takashi sneaks up behind her, intent on stealing a cake right from under her nose. As he is about to make his move, she turns around; only it is not Aya, but Wada the whore. Her flaxlike hair is tied in a bun, making the outline of her skull

Yoji Yamaguchi

stand out in clear relief. She smiles a nearly toothless smile; her gums are blood red. "Two bits for a look, four for a feel, six for a fuck," she yawns. . . .

He is walking down China Alley, on his way to Kikue's. A young girl in a red dress runs out of a hut and grabs his arm. "Please, get me out of here," she implores. He tries to walk away, but she holds fast to his sleeve. "Please help me," she whimpers. He jerks his arm loose and runs; the girl's voice trails behind him: "Wait, come back . . . you can't leave me—Father. . . ."

At Kato's fan-tan table he is on a roll, winning seven games straight. He decides to play one last game and let everything ride on number three. When the dealer begins pulling chips off the table, Takashi already knows he has won. The dealer stops: there are three chips left on the table. Saigo, Kato's man, approaches him. "We can't pay out your money; you broke the bank. You have to choose another prize. You can have this"—Saigo points to Kikue, who has appeared out of nowhere—"or the mansion down the street." He points to a window.

Takashi looks out the window and sees a sprawling castle with a gold roof where China Alley is supposed to be. It looks familiar: it belongs to the beautiful woman.

He studies Kikue. She looks different, younger than he remembers her, her hair jet black and neatly coiffed, nary a wrinkle on her face. She is dressed in a wedding kimono. She stares at him impassively, without recognition. He sees the photo in her hand. Panicked, he says, "I'll take the mansion," and quits the gambling room.

When he arrives at the mansion he enters the main hall,

Face of a Stranger

searching for the woman. He proceeds to the first door he sees and slides it open: in the middle of the room is a mound of shit, a shovel planted upright like a flagstaff in its midst. Even before he hears the voices behind him, he knows whose they are and what they will say: "Chaaarliee . . ."

"Neh, Baka-chan, wake up," a gentle voice interrupted.

Takashi woke with a start. At first he felt like a shipwrecked man reaching land, the comfort of the actual world, where everything made sense. But his relief lasted all of three seconds when he noticed Kikue, sitting at the foot of the bed, staring at him with a worried expression. Her face was back to normal, but she was dressed in strange garb once again, a Western dress this time. He glanced at her hands; the photo she had before was missing.

"Aaah!" he cried, scrambling away from her and curling up with his back to the wall. He clutched a pillow to his chest. "I'm sorry; please forgive me!" he blurted out. "It was nothing personal! I had to choose the mansion; I was there before, in another dream," he babbled, uncertain now whether he was asleep or awake, whether or not Kikue was real.

"What?" Kikue asked, perplexed.

"I know I should have chosen you, but I didn't recognize you in a wedding gown. . . ."

"What are you talking about? Are you all right? What's the matter with you? Are you drunk again?" Her concern hardened into annoyance. Her sharp voice ripped through the air and struck him like slaps to the face, bringing him to his senses.

Takashi relaxed, and let the pillow drop. He peered at her for

Yoji Yamaguchi

a moment, then shook his head. He was awake, after all. But why was she wearing that dress? he wondered.

She sighed impatiently. "Neh, it's a waste of time trying to help you. I never should have come."

"Help me? What are you talking about?"

"Oh, never mind. I don't know what I was thinking."

"What?"

"Forget it. Why don't you go back to sleep? That's all you seem to do."

She rose to her feet and began to pace the room, arms folded, shaking her head. "What a pity. She was perfect for you."

"Who?" Takashi asked.

Kikue reached into her purse and extracted a photograph. "Her," she said, handing it to him.

Takashi studied the photo. She was a young girl of almost perfect beauty; and yet something about her face disturbed him. Then his eyes widened as he recognized her—she was the woman of the mansion. Stunned, and not a little terrified by this uncanny coincidence, he let the photo fall from his hands. "W-who . . . is she?"

Kikue picked up the photo. "Pretty, isn't she?"

"Who is she?" he asked again, louder.

"I knew you'd like her. Too bad she's not for you. I'd let you keep the picture, but I need it."

"Who is she?" he demanded a third time.

"Her name is Kuruzaki Hana. She's on her way to America now, to marry one of you blanket carriers, a guy named Ichimon Nashitaro."

" 'Penniless Boy'?" Takashi frowned skeptically.

Kikue ignored him. "This Ichimon, it seems, has already backed out of the deal, like a coward—only she doesn't know that. When she reaches San Francisco, expecting her husband to greet her, she'll be left all alone on the dock." Kikue shook her head and clucked. "Poor girl. Either she'll be sent back home in disgrace, or worse, Kato or another pimp will get his hands on her."

"What does this have to do with me?"

"I hear the girl comes from a rich merchant family—better still, she's an only child. They're looking for a male heir to inherit their fortune and run the family business. Neh, a man married to her would be set."

Takashi blanched at the second coincidence that cut so close to home. He stared at Kikue with a mixture of suspicion and fear. Was she mocking him, tormenting him with his past? How could she know so much about him?

"Think about it: he wouldn't have to work another day in his life," Kikue was saying. "Too bad for Ichimon that he chickened out."

He stared at her. Was she some kind of medium? Or a witch of some sort? How else was she able to show up quite out of the blue and offer him, literally, the woman of his dreams?

Or was Kikue herself a dream? He remembered the shock of waking up and finding her on top of him the first time. Could that night, and the night after that, have been illusion? What about now? He looked around the room, trying to confirm again whether it was real, whether he was awake.

Kikue threw up her hands in disgust and turned away. "You're so thick-headed! Don't you see: you take Ichimon's place, pretend to be him, and marry her for yourself."

"But . . . but," he stammered, "they're already married!" She sounded real enough to him—real enough to speak to, in any case.

"Only on a piece of paper in Japan. If you marry her here in America, it won't matter."

"But what about his family?"

"He has no family—just like you. He conned her. That's probably why he's backing out: he's afraid of getting caught. So you'd just be one nobody replacing another nobody."

Takashi winced at the way she said *nobody*. "But she won't recognize me from his picture," he blurted out and immediately regretted it. Why did he have to bring up that business? he cursed himself.

Kikue glared at him, taking him aback. Then, to his further discomfort, she burst out laughing.

"What a fool you are! Everybody knows not to trust a picture from America. Don't worry, she won't be too shocked to see you. And besides, I hear Ichimon looks like an ape; you'd be a nice surprise for her."

A troubling thought occurred to him: what if this Ichimon fellow had gotten hold of his picture from Kori? Then he would be posing as Ichimon posing as himself. He would be himself and not himself, original and phony, his own impostor. Takashi shook his head: the whole business was becoming too unreal for him to grasp.

"What's the problem?" Kikue asked. "You've been other people before."

"What do you mean?" Takashi blurted out.

"Neh, you've been a houseboy, a gambler, a field hand too, I bet; you're a monkey man to the Americans, Master Face to the Japanese. Does anybody know who or what you really are?"

She gave him a pitying look. "I tell you, Baka-chan, you'll never be anything in this country until you raise a family. Gamblers are a penny a bushel. You'll always just be a buranke katsugi unless you settle down, make a home, have kids. And where are you going to find a woman like this"—she pointed to the picture—"in Doi's fields? Or maybe inside a bamboo shoot?" She laughed mockingly.

Before he could reply, she knelt beside the bed. "This blanket-carrying life is not for you. You weren't meant to be picking cabbage in a dusty field; a face like yours shouldn't be dripping with sweat and turning brown under the sun. A man like you should be living in a fine house, a regular *hidari-uchiwa*, surrounded by children and servants."

Her voice was beguiling, in a way he'd never heard before. He was nearly overcome by a wave of dizziness, as if intoxicated anew, though not by drink but by Kikue's warmth and sympathy and, most of all, her praise. He began to waver.

"Neh, Baka-chan, here's a beautiful girl, rich beyond your dreams, coming to America looking for a husband. You'll never get another opportunity like this."

Kikue's face seemed to grow hazy as the room began to swim in and out of focus. *Once again you've disappointed,* Takashi heard his brother say, as if he had somehow returned to that dream of so long ago—or perhaps had never awoken from it.

You can't be counted on for the smallest thing, the woman had said, the same woman in the picture, he was now convinced. Had she come back to give him another chance? *You'll never get another opportunity like this.* Was it possible, then, to rectify things, regain all he had lost by his mistakes?

Takashi felt like a man poised to jump from the top floor of a burning building when he heard himself say: "OK. What do I have to do?"

The change in Kikue's demeanor startled him: from temptress to boss in the blink of an eye. She stood up primly and said: "Good. It's settled. Now, I'll need three hundred dollars from you."

"Three hundred dollars?" Takashi gasped. The languor faded, replaced by a harsh lucidity; the meanness of the room reappeared in stark relief.

"Yes. I have to make arrangements, you know, pay certain people, et cetera. You don't want any problems with the Americans, do you? So I'll need the money right away."

"Where will I find three hundred dollars?"

"Ask Doi. He's got money, and he'll do anything for you. He saved your skin from Nakagami, didn't he?"

He might have wondered how she knew that, but at that point he could not be too surprised. "Well, yes, but . . . "

"He'll give it to you. Just promise to pay him back in three months."

"Three months? Three hundred dollars? How am I going to pay him back so quickly?"

"Neh, you're dumb! I told you Kuruzaki Hana comes from a rich family. Once you're married, three hundred dollars will be pocket change to you."

"Oh."

"Ask Doi. I'm sure he'd pay it—just to get rid of you, if nothing else."

Takashi burned with chagrin. He began to think that he was being had. But, no, he thought: the woman's picture. Not even Kori could have arranged to have a picture taken right out of a dream.

"When you get the money, bring it to Nakagami's and give it to the boy Masuji. He'll know what to do," Kikue was saying. "Then, a week from today, go to the Pacific Hotel, early. I'll be there with your new wife. So dress nicely: clean clothes, please. You can wear an American suit as long as it's pressed. All right? That's all." She got up to leave.

He stared at her, nonplussed. Her curt voice sounded as if she were dismissing him like a servant. "Uh . . . "

"Yes?"

The questions sat on his tongue, cumbersome and heavy: *Who are you and why are you doing this for me?* He was desperate to ask, yet afraid of what her answer might be.

"Er, nothing. See you next week."

Because the old man Kimura did not wait for Kikue, Kogoro agreed to drive her back to town. When she climbed into the cab of his truck, she wrinkled her nose: the stench of Kogoro's road kill still clung to the carriage.

Yoji Yamaguchi

Kogoro did not seem to notice, however, and when they were on the road he began to describe the scenery to her like a tour guide. "There's Terao-san's place. His cabbage is starting to come in fine," Kogoro bubbled. "And here comes Ide-san's farm, on the left. He's been having trouble with bugs lately, but his plants look like they'll be all right."

Kikue was not listening. As she stared out the window she did not marvel at the lush, verdant fields, or the gossamerlike clouds scudding across a silky blue sky; no, what struck her more than anything was how isolated each farm was, how far they were from one another. A person could live on one of these farms for a year without seeing another soul. What could it be like for these farmers' wives—not only a world away from home and married to a perfect stranger, but all alone in the middle of nowhere, nothing but rows and rows of cabbage or beets or lettuce for the eye to see?

Maybe they're not so much better off than me, she thought a little sadly. "Don't you get lonely out here?" she asked.

Kogoro, who had been expounding on the qualities of the California soil, was flummoxed by the question. "Uhn? Well . . . no, uh . . . I kinda like being alone, I guess." He blushed and slouched in his seat, like a chastened schoolboy.

They drove in silence for ten minutes. Kikue examined the cab's interior, then turned to inspect the flatbed. "This is a nice truck."

"Uhn? Oh . . . thank you," Kogoro mumbled, still embarrassed.

"I'm glad I could help," she said.

155

"Uhn? Oh, yes, thank you for the loan."

"I wanted to talk to you about it, in fact."

Kogoro jerked his head and gaped at her, eyes widened fearfully, lower lip hanging slack. "What?"

"Your loan."

"Oh, but I'm paying . . ."

She shook her head. "Iya, iya, that's not what I mean. I know you're good for it. But I'm making you an offer. Right now you owe me four hundred dollars. I'll forget it if you do me one favor."

"What?"

"When you get back Arai will ask you to loan him three hundred dollars. I want you to."

"I don't understand."

"Lend Arai three hundred dollars, but on one condition: he must pay you back in ninety days, or else he has to work on your farm for two years—or less, if you decide."

"But . . . but . . ."

"He will of course agree to your terms. But it's important that you make him stick to them. Don't ever let him off the hook! Here." She pulled out a paper from her purse and handed it to him. "I wrote a note that I want you to make him sign."

Kogoro scrutinized the note, his brows cinched tightly. So intent was he on the characters that he did not notice the approaching turn in the road.

"Oh, uh, gomen," Kogoro muttered, unperturbed, and swung the wheel hard left. Kikue lurched and banged her head against the passenger window. As the truck negotiated the bend, she was pressed against the door, half expecting it to fly open and deposit her onto the road.

When the truck reached a straightaway, Kogoro took up the note again. "Ah . . . I don't read so good," he said sheepishly.

Kikue took the paper from his hand. "Here," she said. "I'll read it: 'I, Doi Kogoro, agree to lend Arai Takashi three hundred American dollars. I, Arai Takashi, agree to pay it all back no later than three months from the date of this note. If I do not pay it back in three months, I agree to work in the service of Doi Kogoro at whatever job he chooses for me, for as long as he decides up to but no more than two years.'

"There. What do you think?"

Kogoro was silent for the next mile and a half. Finally, he said: "I can't."

"What?"

"I can't."

"Why not? All you have to do is put up three hundred dollars, and I'll consider your debt paid in full. Even if Arai doesn't pay you back—which he will—you're still saving yourself all that interest."

"But . . ."

"I thought you liked Arai. You're putting him up in your home, after all. Don't you want to help him?"

"Well, yeah. . . ."

"And what about me? This is the thanks I get for helping you buy this truck? This one small favor I ask of you?"

"I don't have the money."

"What?"

Face of a Stranger

"I can't afford three hundred dollars."

"What do you mean? You have the best farm in the county; you're making a fortune. What did you do, lose it all gambling?"

"No, but . . . " He pulled out his own piece of paper from his pocket and handed it to her. "Letter from my brothers," he said.

Kikue held it between her fingers, frowning skeptically. "I don't understand. What does it say?"

"I can't read so good. But I think I didn't send them enough money last time, so they want more. I'll have to give them whatever I can."

"May I . . . ?" She unfolded the letter.

"Sure."

Kikue frowned. Kogoro's brother Ichiro was no scholar; the characters were scrawled and irregular, many of them incorrect. After much effort, she was able to decipher the missive:

What you doing over there addled-head piece of shit? You holding out on us? Why our shares so small? Mother is gone senile and babbles all day. Saburo ran off with the army, will get fool head shot off I'm sure. I come there myself to rip your throat out if you're holding out. If this the best you can do, then get off your ass and start making more! Time for you start contributing good-for-nothing or else just count yourself out of the family.

Kikue felt both anger at Kogoro's arrogant brother and pity at the sight of the helpless giant sitting beside her, his fearful, expectant eyes. At the same time, she did not forget what she was after or what she had to do.

"No, you're wrong, that's not what it says at all," she said. "Listen.

"Thank you very much for your generous monthly gifts. They are easing our burden tremendously. But I must ask you, brother, not to give away all your money to us. Invest it profitably, and indulge yourself from time to time. We all have had a hard life, you more than any of us, so it is right that you should reap some pleasure from your toil. What you give us is more than sufficient. Please, not a penny more. Mother misses you terribly, but she is proud of you and prays nightly for your future success. Saburo has enlisted in the army and is serving honorably. Be well, younger brother. The spirits of our ancestors are smiling on you."

Kogoro beamed; his eyes glistened. Kikue understood that she had struck a nerve somewhere in Kogoro's thick skull, and perhaps for the first time recognized that, like her, he had a story of his own. And now she had interloped in that narrative, in *medias res*, irrevocably altering its outcome with a lie, another pretty lie, and who knew what it could mean to him. She looked away.

On the other hand, she tried to reassure herself, it wasn't likely he'd be seeing his brothers again. So was it so bad for him to be deceived about them, if it made him happy?

Face of a Stranger

Kikue remembered what an old man once said in her hut: *Trust is precious and not to be exploited.* But she didn't ask Doi to trust her; in fact, he should have known better. *Jorō no makoto to shikaku no tamago*—a whore's as honest as an egg is square: isn't that how the saying went? Why was she being so soft? Doi was not her problem, she reminded herself three times. It was her money, after all: he owed her.

"I guess I should write back?" Kogoro asked nervously.

"What? Oh, yes, write them."

"What should I say?"

She raised an eyebrow. "Haven't you ever written them?"

"No."

"Anyone?"

"No." He shook his head glumly. "I can't write so good either."

"Just tell them thanks, and that all is well. Keep it short."

"Oh, but . . . yeah, I guess that's best. How much should I give them?"

"You heard what he wrote: 'not a penny more' than usual."

One can only imagine Kogoro's brothers' reaction when they later received five dollars each and a childishly scrawled letter that read:

Much thanks to Ichiro for kind letter sent. It's good you my brothers. Enclosed fifteen dollars—and "not a penny more."

nine

Shino had not seen Kikue all day, and she was impatient to know what was happening. After pacing in her hut for hours, scaring away all comers with scornful barbs, she decided to look for Kikue at the Pacific Hotel, the Inada bitch be damned.

But she decided not to provoke an incident if she could help it. To that end she put on the ill-fitting second-hand dress, a hideous teal, hoop-skirted affair, given to her by a mission lady who used to visit regularly, long ago. (She stopped coming when she discovered that the women were using the Bibles she handed out as tinder for the braziers in their huts.) Shino had to stuff newspaper in the high-top shoes that went with it to keep them from falling off; even so, her feet were swimming. Finally, she tied her hair back so tight it smarted to its roots.

For Shino these were heady days. Her senses were taut, her mind fairly crackling with excitement. As she walked through the business district, everything around her—the people, streetcar, sun and clouds, birds in the sky—seemed faster, louder, brighter, bigger. Merchants in shirtsleeves and aprons, matronly women in their American dresses—they no longer annoyed her but now filled her with wonder, as if they were a spectacle she was beholding for the first time.

She was giddy—and not so much at the prospect of tricking Arai, though she was certainly eager for that. More important to her was the sense that, for the first time since coming to America and maybe the first time in her life, she was able to control events, determine matters—not only hers, but those of others as well, namely Arai's: in short, do rather than be done to.

No, she really did not have it in for Arai; when he abandoned her in China Alley that night, she felt more disgust than anger; and she was hardly surprised. Kikue was a different story.

Shino did not fail to notice her friend's doggedness, her fussing over trifling details, and most of all the exaggerated importance she was placing on what amounted to little more than a practical joke. In Shino's eyes, Kikue was acting more and more like one who had been jilted.

She wondered if it was possible that, after all they had been through, Kikue could still be enamored of that face. Shino herself had never felt that way: the first time she saw his picture, she thought he was too pretty for her liking. She tried to imagine him lying naked on the bed in Kikue's hut; it did nothing for her.

162

When we pull off our trick she will watch his eyes bulge and his jaw drop like an idiot's, and see what he really looks like, Shino reassured herself.

As she walked past the church, something caught her eye. She stopped. It was Inada the innkeeper, leaving the church, slouching noticeably, a forlorn look on his face. He plodded slowly in the direction of his hotel.

What's his problem? she wondered. She had never paid much mind to the church or its members; but her curiosity was piqued. She wanted to find out what had laid uppity Inada so low. She glanced around, then walked into the church as casually as she could.

Inside, four crude wooden benches bracketed a middle aisle; a rickety lectern stood at the far end. Sitting on the first row of benches with their backs to the door were two well-dressed women and a man dressed in black.

"Poor Sumi-san," one of the women was saying. "Having to endure her husband's mistress living in her home, under the pretense of sanctuary. Unspeakable!"

"Neh," the other woman said, "I can't believe Inada-san would do such a thing. He is such a nice man and, what's more, he knows the Gospels by heart, every chapter and verse. No, no, it's simply not possible."

"His story is unbelievable. Whoever heard of a prostitute lending money at interest? And if he needed money, why didn't he just join a tanomoshi?"

The man spoke up; his voice was adenoidal, boyish. "Surely the woman has used her charms to insinuate herself in Inada-san's household. No doubt the story of his debt to her is her creation. Such is the guile of loose women."

"And men like Kato," the older woman added. "I'm sure he is profiting off this somehow."

"Oh, that horrible man!" the younger woman squealed. "The sound of his name makes my skin crawl!"

"So," the man grunted again. "I am glad that Mrs. Inada came to us and told us the whole story. Now we can take appropriate steps."

Shino leaned forward and strained to hear: something was afoot.

"It is imperative that we remove the prostitute from the premises before the fifteenth," the man said. "It will not do if she is there that day."

The older woman asked: "Sensei, what do you think the prostitute will do when she's evicted?"

Shino bit her lip to keep from bellowing. Kikue has been betrayed—by that mouse of a man and his warthog of a wife! She wanted to run off and warn her friend, but she needed to hear more.

"What can she do? Sumiko-san has told us everything: she can no longer blackmail Inada-san. Alas, that he was so fearful of our censure! As if we were so unforgiving! But nothing will happen to him. After all, he is not the only man in our congregation who has, er, succumbed to temptation."

At this the younger woman let out an ear-piercing wail that made Shino jump. "Neh, Sensei," the older woman hissed. "Her husband—remember?"

"Ah, but that was so long ago," he protested. "Please excuse me, Urusaki-san." His voice was choked with embarrassment.

Abruptly, the woman named Urusaki stopped crying and said brightly: "Oh, that's all right, Sensei. All of that went on in his previous life."

"Uhn?"

"Before he was reborn a Christian, I mean."

"Oh, of course."

"So you don't think the prostitute will be a problem?" the older woman asked.

"Not at all. In fact, soon we will be rid of them all—including that fellow Kato. Hayashi-san, I have a promise that this will be done from the subdeputy adjutant to the consul general himself—not to mention the mayor as well."

"Huh," she sniffed. "The consulate and the Americans haven't lifted a finger against these amegoro. What makes you think they'll start now?"

"That's not so! Why, just last year, you'll remember, the chargé d'affaire's number two aide came all the way from San Francisco to attend our demonstration against Kato and his gang."

"Oh, I remember that!" Mrs. Urusaki enthused. "It was such a lovely spring day! And after the rally we had a picnic, right behind the church. Hatsue-san made her wonderful osushi— oh, I almost couldn't stop myself—oh, and Rei-chan, do you remember? Your little girl ate so much American *aiisu kureemu* she got sick and you had to take her home early. . . ."

Shino leaned against the door frame. So, she thought, they mean to run all of us out of town, not just Kikue. What would that mean for her? Beg for a living on the road, sell myself to another Kato in another place, well out of these do-gooders' sight? Maybe they'd send me to Montana, fill my head with their religion. *Iya;* might as well throw in my lot with Kato, help him thwart these people however I can, and go on working for him in peace.

But no. She knew that she could hope for nothing better than to see Kato fall, whether at the hands of these people or some other way. She would be able to take care of herself, come what may.

"Er, can we help you?" The man's voice rang clear across the room, and Shino realized she had been discovered. As they rose from their pew and approached her, she cursed herself under her breath.

An unlikelier trio she had never seen before. Urusaki, the flighty one, towered over all of them, a giantess with shoulders that seemed as broad as Shino was tall. Her hair was styled in the Western fashion, and parted to one side. The older woman, Hayashi, was reed thin, with a long, bony face, large, wide-set eyes, and a slightly puckered mouth. She was not old—no more than forty—but her hair was streaked with gray.

Perhaps most startling was the *sensei.* With his soft, cherubic face, he looked almost as young as Shino, and standing between the statuesque Mrs. Urusaki and the gaunt Mrs. Hayashi, he cut a squat, gnomelike figure; his arms and legs seemed to be of exactly equal length. But what Shino noticed right away was his blockish, oversize head. The jowly cheeks and double chin looked as if they had squashed his neck down into his shoulders.

166

"Welcome," he said, his adenoidal voice sounding vaguely flustered. "I am Onara. I'm the minister of this church." He gave a curt bow.

"I am *Gloria* Urusaki," the giant woman interjected. "I was born Sachiko, but changed it to *Gloria* when we came to this country. My husband, *George*—he runs a barbershop on Second Street—he changed his name, too, of course—he used to be Kunitaro—his family's from Kanagawa Prefecture, where there are quite a few missions opening up these days, I hear—and he insisted we both take on Western names. 'An American given name and a Japanese surname—for our new home and our old,' he said. It's difficult to pronounce, neh? I had such a time learning it myself!" Mrs. Urusaki laughed gaily. Shino frowned.

"Can we help you?" Hayashi echoed the reverend.

Shino was taken aback; she half-expected a greeting more like the one she received from Mrs. Inada—hostile, arrogant, insulting. Instead, these people were downright cordial to her. Then it occurred to her: they didn't know who she was; the dress had fooled them. She could pass herself off as anyone—anyone but a prostitute.

The anonymity made her feel mischievous. "Eh, sorry to bother you," she said as timidly as she could. "But could you tell me how to find the Pacific Hotel?"

Mrs. Hayashi told her. Onara asked: "Have you just arrived in this country?"

Shino tried to smile bashfully. "Hai. My husband has been living in America for some time, and at last he's sent for me."

"Oh, how nice!" Mrs. Urusaki bubbled. "So, you're going to meet him at the hotel. Does he live there?"

"Yes—actually, he owns it."

"*Nan da?*" Onara gasped as the two women gawked at her, wide-eyed and slack-jawed with astonishment and horror. "W-who do you mean?"

"My husband—Inada Masajiro. If you see him, please tell him I'm here. Well, thanks for your help. Good-bye." She turned and walked out the door, barely able to suppress her laughter.

In the church, Mrs. Urusaki moaned, clapped her hand to her forehead, and began to sway precariously on her feet. Onara stepped up and tried to brace her but could not stop her from collapsing; instead, she fell on top of the smaller man, sending both of them to the floor in a heap.

Decked in a black dress that hid her feet, with a hat and veil to match, gliding through downtown, door to door, Kikue looked like a spirit come calling, as one man would recall; or, as another put it later, like the devil come to separate the damned from the saved.

In fact, she came offering grace. With her collection of promissory notes in hand, she visited every one of her debtors, giving each man the chance to pay back half of what he owed; she would forgive him the rest (plus any interest). For those who declined her offer, she planned to sell their obligations to Kato. (She did not inform them of that jeopardy, of course.)

Yet, of the twelve men she visited, only Nakagami took advantage of her deal. Likely it was her appearance that gave the others pause. Who would accept terms that sounded too good to be true from a woman who looked like a demon?

The only person she did not call on was Inada. When Shino finally found her at the hotel and told her of the plans to evict her, Kikue was not surprised. She knew that, sooner or later, his wife would have her way.

"But it's not the bitch," Shino protested. "It's that guy Onara."

"No, she just doesn't want to embarrass her husband. So she's gotten this priest to tell him what to do. Inada won't mind obeying him so much as he would obeying her."

When Kikue had moved in, no more was said of Inada's original debt. He thinks he's in the clear just because he lets me that room, she thought as she arrived at Kato's restaurant. Could he imagine that I would do what I'm going to do— namely, sell his hide to Kato?

Though Shino's news did not throw Kikue into a panic, she was puzzled by the importance of the date they had set to throw her out. She wondered what was so important about that day, how her presence would ruin their plans. She resolved to herself: *If Kato lets me down here, I'll be sure to be in the hotel on the fifteenth, priest or no priest.*

Signs of the times: not only did she enter the empty restaurant unmolested, she had to wait a good three minutes before anyone emerged. Chairs were strewn about the room carelessly, the tables and floor were covered with dust, and all was utterly still: she thought the place had been abandoned. She was almost ready to leave when a boy, no more than sixteen, plodded in, carrying a bent knife and a bruised, shriveled orange. He did not seem even to notice her. When she asked to see Kato, he glanced dully at her and paused just long enough to jerk his head toward the door from which he had emerged before settling down at one of the tables.

As she walked through the kitchen, Kikue saw brown, moldy vegetable rinds scattered on the greasy floor, where roaches scurried in all directions. She pulled up the hem of her good, clean dress, and stepped gingerly.

Though it had been years since Kikue had last seen the office of Kato, the change in its appearance startled her. The shelves along the walls were empty but for three sacks of flour and a scattering of tin cans covered with cobwebs. The cheap ornaments and wall decorations were gone. The top of the great oak desk was bare but for the half-empty bottle of Scotch standing like a lighthouse in the middle of a desolate sea.

Kato was dozing in his chair. He was even fatter than before. A lock of his gray hair hung over his forehead like an overgrown weed. His round, wire-rimmed glasses had slid off his nose and hung crookedly from one ear. His tan suit was badly wrinkled, with a few grains of rice stuck to the lapels, and a dark stain— probably from the whiskey—just below his right breast pocket. He wore no tie, and his shirt collar, rumpled and stained a dull yellow, was unbuttoned.

The last time Kikue stood before him in that basement she had been angry and bewildered; now she felt nothing but disgust and wonder—wonder at his dominion over her, whereby he could feed or not feed her, clothe or not clothe her, house or

170

Yoji Yamaguchi

not house her; allow or not allow her to live. Whence came the power of this fat, rumpled man sleeping like a baby (and beginning to drool like one as well) before her? She thought of Saigo—young, strong, cold-blooded Saigo: why did he take orders from someone as soft and weak as Kato? Why did any of them? The disgust she felt for Kato rebounded to her. If Kato was a pathetic old man, what did that make her?

Unceremoniously she kicked the front of the desk. Kato's head jerked up; his glasses slid off and bounced off his belly. With a deftness of reflex that could only have been conditioned with much practice, he snatched them with his right hand and replaced them onto his nose.

The sight of her face—on which he had not laid eyes in four years—did not startle Kato in the least. He seemed just as bored as the fellow upstairs. Kikue had expected him angrily to demand to know her business, upbraid her, throw her out, or (in the worst case) call in Saigo to deal with her. Instead, he merely yawned, dug a finger into his ear, shifted uncomfortably in his chair to scratch his balls, and inquired meekly: "Oh. Which one are you?"

For an instant Kikue felt something close to pity for the old man. Gone from his voice was the pomp, the chilly, sonorous ring. Now he seemed to be just another old man whose grand plans of fortune had been reduced to a bottle of whiskey and a few sacks of meal on the shelf. As Kato stared at her curiously, she began to falter. The speech she had prepared on her way to the restaurant fled her, so she blurted out artlessly: "I want to be released."

Face of a Stranger

Whatever sympathy she might have felt for him dissipated at the sound of his wheezy laughter. "Really? Well, good for you," he snickered, bowing his head mockingly.

Stung, Kikue pulled a handful of notes from her pocketbook and flung them on his desk. Kato stopped laughing and stared at her, puzzled.

"Here's my deal," she said tersely. "You let me go, and these are all yours."

Kato frowned and fingered the heap of papers tentatively. "What is this?" he asked.

"IOUs," she said, "and good ones, too—not like those worthless things you get from the losers at your gambling tables. These come from locals, people who aren't going anywhere. They'll pay you with interest, without fail. I hold them now, and I'll trade them for the money I owe you. You can make more from these notes in one month than you could get from us in six.

"What's more," she added, "some of them belong to the people who want to shut you down. Maybe they'll leave you alone if they find out they owe you."

Kato looked at her skeptically and not a little apprehensively, clearly uncertain whether she was lying or merely insane. "You don't believe me? How do you think I afforded this?" she challenged, tugging the neckline of her dress.

Kato glowered at her. "You've been skimming off me," he fumed.

"Huh—Junzo's an idiot, but he's not that dumb." Kikue sniffed. Kato winced at the mention of his nephew. "You can only skim so much, I mean."

Kato looked thoroughly discomfited. He hunched over and

squinted at each note. "The handwriting's different on each," he murmured.

"Of course," she said impatiently. "Do you think I wrote all these? Do I have eight hands like an octopus?"

Kato leaned back in his chair and folded his hands over his paunch. "So I get all this debt if I let you go?" he asked bemusedly.

"Plus five hundred dollars, so I can get away from this place. And I don't want your goons coming after me," she snapped.

"What's to stop the rest from trying to leave?"

"Why stop them? We're not making you rich."

Kato looked aghast. "Impossible. I'd be a laughingstock."

Kikue batted her eyes. "Excuse me, boss, but I think it's too late to worry about that."

The fat man struggled out of his chair and to his feet, and slammed the desk. "You're mocking me?" he growled.

"Not at all. But I already hear someone from out of town is going to buy out Onishi's flophouse and turn it into a brothel," she lied.

Kato gaped at her. His body sagged, and he had to lean heavily on the desk. Then he looked up at her and curled his lip wickedly. "What's to stop me from selling the lot of you to this person?" he sneered.

"How much do you think you'll get for used goods like us? Will you get a good price for Wada, that corpse? Or what about that girl stuck on Angel Island?" she taunted.

"How did you know about her?"

"Everybody knows about her! Like I said, boss, it's too late for you to worry about face."

173

Kato stared at her dumbly. He fell back into his chair; air whooshed out of the cushions and the legs creaked ominously.

"'The number one gold mine in the world' they call this place," he muttered distractedly, "'the land of opportunity.' *Chikusho!* I came here to make a fortune, I had it, greatness was in my grasp. Now I'm reduced to haggling with whores." He grunted, then sighed dramatically.

Kikue laughed. "What greatness? Even if you weren't a pimp and a thug, or if you weren't up to your neck in debts, you'd still be nobody in this country. How can you be a big shot when you can't even own property? Important men live wherever they please, not just where the hakujin *allow* them. And on the day when the Americans come and take away all you've got, round you up like a dog, and ship you off—back to Japan, or maybe even out in the middle of the desert—do you think they'll bow and scrape and call you 'otono'? Ha!

"Face it—in the hakujin eyes, you're no better than me; neither are those blowhard Christians, for that matter. We're all the same to the Americans. So it makes no difference if I'm the one making you a deal instead of some moneylender or some big shot at the Keihin Bank."

Kato flipped through the notes with a trembling hand. "I'll cancel your debt, but I won't give you any money."

"Kechinbo da na!" she said disgustedly. "These notes are worth more money than I ever owed you."

"Who knows if they're worth anything at all. All right, twenty-five dollars."

"Four hundred."

"Ridiculous. Thirty dollars."

"Three hundred and fifty."

"You're beginning to irritate me. Fifty dollars, and no more."

"I'll tell you what: cancel Shino's debt along with mine, and these are all yours. No money down."

"Shino? You mean that ugly little girl with the big mouth, who's always giving my nephew a hard time? The one Saigo likes to fuck?"

So that's where she gets her information, Kikue thought, chagrined. She bristled at Kato's description of her friend but did not want to ruin the negotiations; she was too close to success. "So," she replied.

"Ridiculous! Now you're robbing me!"

"Neh, boss, let me ask you: have any of your girls ever paid off their debts in full?"

Kato frowned and looked away. "Of course not," Kikue answered herself. "They all grow old before their time, like Wada, and die before they can earn you back your money. No wonder you lose so much each year! You ought to cut your losses, get out of this business, and stick to gambling and usury, neh? Think of all the money you'd save!"

Kato drummed his fingers on the top of his desk, staring at the pile of notes before him, mulling Kikue's words. After what seemed like hours to her, he picked up one of the notes and read it. "Who's . . . I-I-Inada?"

Were she still able to, she might have wept for joy.

ten

Kikue's visit had a miraculous effect on Takashi. Not long after she left, his fever broke, color returned to his complexion, and he was ravenous. When Kogoro returned from town, he found Takashi in the kitchen helping himself to a pile of scrambled eggs.

Diffidently, Kogoro presented him with the note Kikue had drafted for him. As she predicted, Takashi agreed, though not without reservations.

"A note?" he said incredulously. "You want me to sign an IOU?"

Kogoro was too embarrassed to reply; he could only nod.

Takashi examined the paper. "You wrote this?"

Kogoro blushed: Kikue had sworn him to silence about her part. "Hai," he gulped and nodded his head.

Takashi frowned as he read the note; then, to Kogoro's surprise, he burst out laughing. "I have to work for you if I don't repay you in time? Ha ha ha! OK. What do I care? In three months I'll be buying farms, not working them." Kogoro was baffled as he watched his friend sign his name with a jaunty flourish. Kogoro's hand was trembling so much when he scribbled his name in the plain phonetic script that KO-GO-RO looked more like FU-BU-zero.

Kikue had not told him why Takashi needed so much money. When Takashi told him the news of his imminent marriage, Kogoro could not believe it. It was all so sudden, so out of the blue. The idea of marriage was incomprehensible to him. To call a woman wife, spend one's whole life with her . . .

"Who is she?" Kogoro asked.

"Her name is Kuruzaki Hana," Takashi replied, and reeled off her life history and her family background, as provided to him by Kikue. "And she's the most beautiful woman you'll ever see. Just you wait."

"Oh, uh . . . is she nice?"

The way Takashi rolled his eyes and curled his lip told Kogoro that he had just asked a very stupid question. Only then did he understand that Takashi had never met the woman. Marriage is bad enough, but to a perfect stranger? The thought terrified him.

Kogoro withdrew the money from his bank account and handed it over to Takashi, who made his way directly to Nakagami's. There, as instructed, he gave it to Masuji. Kogoro expected that his friend would want to stay for a few rounds at least; to his shock, Takashi insisted on returning to the farm straightaway.

In the ensuing week, Takashi had not a drop to drink; rather, to Kogoro's further astonishment, he offered to help around the farm. "Maybe I'll get a farm of my own, or maybe I'll end up working for you," he said jovially.

His humor changed considerably as soon as they got busy. Already soft from his stint as a domestic, still weak from the flu and his drinking, he was in no shape to work side by side with Kogoro. At the end of the first day his back was aching so much that he could barely climb into the bathtub or squat on the privy. Kogoro was not a taskmaster; quite the contrary, he did his best to keep Takashi from working himself to death. But it was his very concern for him—as well as the preternatural energy and cheerful resignation with which he labored—that seemed to drive Takashi into a frenzy of industry quite uncharacteristic of him and quite regrettable: for mishap is inevitable for a clod with a zealous heart.

When Takashi saw Kogoro effortlessly shouldering fence posts four at a time, he was determined to follow suit, and wound up on his back, pinned down under a pile of lumber. The next day he tried to glaze one of the windows and promptly shattered three brand-new panes of glass. The third day he knocked himself over backward trying to crank the churlish tractor motor.

Takashi's revival was a mixed blessing for Kogoro: on the one hand, he was happy to see his friend active and well, no longer a rambling, eerie wreck; on the other hand, as a worker he was calamitous; his very touch was havoc. Ill-adapted to the farm life, his appetite became insatiable, and it was all Kogoro could

179

do to keep his pantries stocked. But Kogoro's usually simple fare—of the rice and cabbage variety—was not satisfactory to him: he wanted steaks, hams, roast duck, thick steaming stews; rich pastries or succulent ices for desert. By the end of the week, and after five visits to the bank to withdraw money, Kogoro was almost as eager for the wedding as Takashi himself.

The day of Takashi's assignation arrived. Kogoro drove him to town and dropped him off at the Pacific Hotel, dressed in his only usable suit, a black linen with creases sharp enough to cut paper. Takashi wanted to meet his new wife alone, so Kogoro agreed to come back in an hour to take them to the local Buddhist temple for the ceremony that Kikue said she had arranged. The day was fine, so he decided to walk around town.

His sluggish mind was working full tilt to reckon with the fact that he might have to borrow against next year's earnings—something he had not done in two years and had hoped he would never have to do again. And after the next harvest, what next? he wondered. Would he have to borrow against the following crop, and so on—always in debt, always an early frost or drought away from losing his farm, losing everything? Even as he trudged under an infinite blue sky in the middle of day, he felt cramped, cribbed in; his chest tightened, and he broke out in a sweat. Though he was in fact still better off than ninety percent of the immigrant farmers in the state, he nonetheless felt the desperation of a man on the brink of ruin.

He was so lost in thought that he nearly stumbled over the man kneeling on the sidewalk in his path. It was Yamada the

180

Yoji Yamaguchi

grocer, wailing hysterically. His clerk Nishitake was kneeling at his side, trying to hoist him to his feet. Tiny shards of glass lay on the ground, twinkling in the sunlight. Kogoro was mystified by the scene until he noticed the front of Yamada's store. The show windows had been thoroughly shattered, the door ripped off one of its hinges. Kogoro peered inside and saw a young boy picking himself off the floor and shaking his head groggily. Blood was trickling from a cut above his eye.

"I'm ruined, I'm ruined!" Yamada was crying. "That whore, that bitch, sold me out to Kato! Chikusho!"

"Kato! Danidachi! Bloodsucker!" Nishitake screeched to the heavens. "Stop preying on your own kind! We are your people! Leave us alone!"

Kogoro panicked at the sight of such misery and chaos. His instinct was to stoop down and help the distraught pair on the ground; at the same time, he wanted to flee. Then he remembered Takashi. He did not know whence or why the revelation came to him at that moment, but he had no doubt it was true: Takashi was walking into a trap. With both shame and relief, Kogoro hustled off, leaving Yamada to mourn the wreckage of his dream.

When his uncle charged Junzo with leading Saigo and two other men on what he called "a vital mission"—terrorizing his newly acquired debtors—both of them expected something to go wrong. And yet for most of the morning Junzo and his men carried out their task without a hitch. With the precision of a well-trained army they charged through town, paying calls on

Face of a Stranger

Yamada's store, Ishida's flower shop, Kobayashi's laundry, Kanemura's noodle place, and Shinda's funeral home. Gleefully they smashed windows, broke furniture, and roughed up anyone in sight, giving the people a taste of Kato's penalties for late or nonpayment of debts.

Though Junzo did not participate in any of the actual mischief (his uncle expressly forbade it), that did not diminish his pleasure in the least. To snap his fingers and then stand by and watch Saigo and his men go to work filled him with a rush of power. He felt almost as if the thugs were his appendages; his heart raced and he began to pant, and as they swung their clubs and two-by-fours and kicked their hapless victims on the ground, he could almost feel the shock of the blows running up his arms and legs. When they laughed and taunted the shopkeepers, a giddiness swept over him as if he were being tickled, and—he could not help it—he began to get hard. And when those who had mocked and cursed him at his arrival cried for mercy, the feeling was even sweeter.

Gone for the moment was the fear he had known all his life. With Saigo and the others at his beck and call, he felt that he could stand up to any man—or woman, for that matter: he had sorely wished to call on all those nasty whores who had treated him no better than a dog ever since he set foot in town, to show them a thing or two. How weak, stupid, or cowardly would he look to them with his muscle at his side? he wondered. But his uncle had forbidden such action, so there was nothing to be done.

He strutted through town like a conquering general, with his

Yoji Yamaguchi

little army trailing ten paces behind. His only regret was that his mother was not there to see him, though he was certain that his uncle would commend him to her well. Junzo was grateful to his uncle for entrusting him with the job, and the prospect of reporting their success made him tremble with anticipation.

But, alas, all of his hopes crashed, and his newly found courage fled him like sparrows lighting from a tree. Their last stop was supposed to have been Inada's rooming house, and to Junzo's chagrin he realized that in the excitement of their violent spree he had forgotten the address, which his uncle had told him, not once, but three times. None of them had any clue where it was or what it looked like. His little army was lost.

As Saigo and the others glared at him mutinously, Junzo felt an urgent need to shit. A maelstrom of violent images and sounds—glass shattering, wood cracking, the thuds of boots and clubs upon flesh, cries of pain, wicked laughter—whirled through his head, and he concluded that these men were quite insane. What was he doing alone with them, he wondered, without his uncle around to control them? He was not like them; he was not meant for such work. Why did his uncle put him in such a fix? Why did his mother send him to America? At the moment all he wanted was to be left alone.

Then, a stroke of luck for Junzo: he spotted Takashi about a hundred feet away, in front of Inada's hotel. "Ho!" Junzo cried. "Look at the guy in the fancy suit! I bet he's one of those Christian types. Let's rough him up! It would make my uncle happy!"

Saigo and the others reacted like baited dogs, tugging at their

Face of a Stranger

leashes. "Ehh," Saigo hissed. "We'll beat him up and show these people who runs this town." Coolly, deliberately, he stalked off toward Takashi, and the others followed.

Junzo felt the power resurging in him. "Go get him, boys!" he piped cheerfully, hastening after the men, though not too quickly lest he close the distance between them.

Mrs. Inada felt like falling to her knees and giving thanks to God. All was well: her husband's transgressions were finally made right; a woman was rescued from a life of sin; and, perhaps most important, the harlot was gone for good.

She felt as if she had been tested, like Job, and survived, her state of grace intact. When her husband first informed her of his illicit deal with the harlot Kikue, it was worse than her worst fears. To think, she and her daughters had been living in a hotel acquired by the ill-gotten proceeds of the flesh trade. She felt debased, unclean—and it was all her husband's fault.

To make matters worse, he was bringing another girl into the hotel. Though she was coming with the Reverend Onara's blessing—indeed, at his request—Mrs. Inada could not help but feel that their hotel was viewed by the righteous as little better than a brothel, a way station for whores.

When she could endure her shame no longer, she went to Onara and told him all. Onara intoned: *"'I saw Satan fall like lightning from heaven. And I have given you the power to tread underfoot snakes and scorpions, and all the forces of the enemy.'* The woman is an abomination, an unclean spirit possessing your household. Send your husband to me," he said, puffing out his chubby chest. "And I will bid him to cast her hence."

Mrs. Inada relayed the reverend's message to her husband and informed him: "She can do nothing to us now. I've told everyone of your disgrace. Let her proclaim it to the heavens, for all I care."

When he trudged upstairs to give Kikue the bad news, he found the room emptied of her belongings. A note was pinned to the door.

Thanks for your hospitality. You don't owe me a thing now.

Kikue

"Well, what did you expect?" Mrs. Inada clucked when he reported this strange coincidence. "These whores have no manners. She's probably found a better place to sell herself. A regular *iden*."

"Sumiko! Such talk," Inada scolded weakly. Mrs. Inada laughed. She could not remember the last time she had been in such good spirits. For her part, she was pleased that the harlot at least had the decency to leave in a discreet manner—and none too soon, for the same day Kikue left, the woman Hana Kuruzaki arrived from Angel Island, thanks to the intervention of the Japanese consulate.

When Hana was brought to the hotel by Onara, Hayashi, and Urusaki, Mrs. Inada treated her with all the kindness she could muster. And yet, like a discordant note in an otherwise perfect hymn, she could not help but notice the girl's haughty disdain for all of them, and her seeming ingratitude and indifference to their efforts on her behalf. Though the people at the consulate mentioned the girl's instability, Mrs. Inada was not so sure. Hana seemed to be nothing if not in full possession of herself.

Another disturbance was the puzzling story Mrs. Hayashi relayed to her, of the mysterious woman claiming to be Inada's new wife. Had she heard it from Mrs. Urusaki, Mrs. Inada would have ignored it. But since Mrs. Hayashi reported it, and Reverend Onara later confirmed it, she could not dismiss it so easily. Of course she did not believe that the woman was in fact her husband's second wife. More likely she was connected to the harlot somehow, sent to make mischief on her behalf—though to what end, Mrs. Inada could not fathom.

There was no need for her to confront her husband about it, as her victory over him was already complete. Thoroughly crushed and humiliated, Inada plodded through the lobby like a tired old man. Even as he trudged past the desk on his way to their basement room without looking at her, she was making plans to bring Imoyaro in to help her run the hotel.

Takashi swept into the inn. "Hello!" he called out cheerfully as he sauntered to the desk.

"Irrashaimase," Mrs. Inada replied brightly, with a fervent bow. And so the Lord succors the righteous, she thought. What luck! No sooner were they rid of that whore, the bane of her life, than a new guest—and a quite handsome one at that!—comes along. She beamed at the charming gentleman.

"I'm here to meet someone," he announced grandly.

"Of course," Mrs. Inada said, bowing demurely. "May I ask the Guest the name of the party he wishes to see?"

"Her name is Kikue."

The smile vanished from Mrs. Inada's face, replaced by a frown as hard as granite. "Who?" she snapped.

"Kikue . . . " Takashi realized for the first time that he did not know her last name; he wondered if she even had one.

Mrs. Inada grabbed the nearest weapon she could find, a rug beater, and brandished it menacingly. "Out! Out of this place! This is not a brothel! Filthy whoremonger! Good-for-nothing! Your strumpet doesn't live here anymore! Vile man! Out!"

Takashi gaped at the woman. "What? Live here? Kikue? What do you mean? Wait . . . you don't . . . I'm not here for that. . . . Stop swinging that! . . . She's my go-between."

Mrs. Inada lowered her arm and peered at him quizzically. "What's that?"

"She's my nakaodo."

Mrs. Inada raised the rug beater behind her ear and shook it angrily. "Nonsense! A whore brokering a marriage? You expect me to believe that?"

"It's true," Takashi squealed plaintively. "She told me to come here to meet my new wife."

"And who's that?"

"Her name is Kuruzaki Hana."

The rug beater fell from Mrs. Inada's hand and she staggered back two steps. Her jaw flexed noiselessly four times before she was able to stammer: *D-d-dare ka?*

"Kuruzaki Hana."

"But . . . how did you know she . . . who . . . " She had been told that the girl's case was strictly confidential.

"I told you: Kikue arranged it. Anyway, Kuruzaki Hana is the one I came to see. She's going to be my wife. She's staying here, yes?"

Takashi underwent a frightening metamorphosis in Mrs. Inada's eyes. No longer handsome, his narrow face, sharp nose, his preposterously cut suit, and, most of all, his thin-lipped smirk—all of these gave him the look of a serpent. Then, to her horror, it dawned on her: standing before her was one of Kato's men in cahoots with the whore Kikue, come to abduct the girl and take her off into a life of whoredom.

Scared as she was, she could not let that happen without a struggle. *For whosoever tries to save his life will lose it.* She screamed, as if to expel the fear building inside and clutching her guts, picked up the cudgel and began to fillip Takashi on the head. "Oh no you don't! You amegoro are not getting this one! She's a child of God now! So get out! Get out! Maybe the Lord will forgive you if you leave quietly; otherwise, I'll have to smash your head in."

"Ouch! Ow! What's wrong? What'd I . . . I don't understand."

"Go to those whores in that disgusting alley. Stay away from our place!" She stepped out from behind the desk, flailing away.

Takashi cried out in confusion and pain, turned tail and fled toward the door. He did not see Saigo or his two men, who had just burst in, standing just inside the threshold. When he ran headlong into the trio, they were too surprised to beat him as planned. Takashi, for his part, was nonplussed at seeing the

Yoji Yamaguchi

bouncer from the gambling den in the Pacific Hotel, of all places. The four men stared at one another dumbly.

An angry shriek caused them all to whirl in the direction of Mrs. Inada. "More thugs!" she shouted. "How many of your friends did you bring, eh?" With each word she bellowed, her courage grew. "Four men? It takes four of you amegoro to handle one poor defenseless girl? Cowards: shame on you."

As the three new villains exchanged bewildered glances, Mrs. Inada's heart was racing and her head burned as if on fire. She felt as if she were no longer in possession of herself but seized by some spirit above and beyond her. She wondered if the exhilaration she was feeling was anything akin to the ecstasy of the apostles, as she dropped her rug beater and grabbed a vase from the lobby table to fling at the invaders.

Her throw went high and wide, smashing into the window of the front door. Glass and china shards sprayed over the men, the lobby, the stoop outside. Cowering in the face of the woman's apparent madness, cradling their heads with their arms, Takashi, Saigo, and the other two men tried to back out the door all at once, creating a logjam.

Mrs. Inada picked up her rug beater and advanced on the four men, who were grappling one another trying to extricate themselves. The door leading to the basement opened: it was Inada. "Sumiko, what was that noise? Did something break?" he asked.

At the sound of her husband's voice, the spirit seemed to flee Mrs. Inada. She looked at him, then at the frightened queue at the door. She frowned at the broken window, puzzled; then she blinked rapidly, several times, as if coming out of a dream.

"Inada-san, what is going on?" a tremulous voice asked. It was Tsushida, poking his head through the half-open door to the dining room.

"Inada?" a voice squeaked from the entrance. It was Junzo. Everyone turned to see the pudgy, potato-faced boy standing outside the threshold, hopping up and down behind the four men. He was panting heavily; his pallid, flaccid face was beaded with sweat from running just to keep his men within view.

"Get out of my way, let me in," he whined. Saigo and the other two rolled their eyes and scowled, yielding but a hand's width of space for him to slither through. Even Takashi, who had no idea who Junzo was, frowned as he stumbled past him.

"You're Inada? Oh, what luck!" Junzo chirped happily.

Inada took his place beside his wife and stared at the sweaty, slight fellow. "That is me. How can I help you?" he inquired.

"Oh, my uncle will be so happy with me!" Junzo bubbled, practically dancing with excitement. "I can't believe it! What a relief!"

"Eh, what can I do for you?" Inada asked.

"Oh, ho, not for me! For you! What you can do for you!" Junzo piped.

Mr. and Mrs. Inada exchanged baffled looks. "I don't understand," Inada said, his voice grave with concern. Junzo seemed to be quite out of his wits.

Junzo fumbled in his coat pocket, pulled out a slip of paper, dropped it on the floor, picked it up, unfolded it, and at last presented it triumphantly, though upside down, to the couple.

"What is this?" Inada asked patiently.

Yoji Yamaguchi

"Your note," Junzo said. "The whore Kikue lent you money that wasn't hers. She stole it from my uncle."

"Kikue?" Inada said. Mrs. Inada gasped. From the corner of her eye she noted that Tsushida had disappeared—no doubt to spread the word to the congregation, prattling old man. More humiliation at the hands of the harlot! She thought, outraged: Such is the treachery of a whore.

Junzo warbled: "So now you owe him, and you better pay up! If you don't, this is what you can expect!" He cleared his throat, threw back his shoulders, raised his right hand, and snapped his fingers.

Junzo had been so pleased to find Inada that he failed to notice his men backing away from the door, paying him and the Inadas no heed. He turned and saw at the door the massive frame of a giant that seemed to fill the entire doorway.

Kogoro peered at the scene before him curiously. Mrs. Inada cried out: "Help us, sir! These men are trying to extort money from us and kidnap one of our guests. And he's the leader!" She pointed a finger at Junzo.

Junzo squawked: "I'm not! I . . . I just came here to collect . . . for my uncle. My uncle! He sent me here!" His chin began to quiver, and he looked ready to cry.

Kogoro could scarcely believe it: his premonition was right, after all; he had come just in time to rescue Takashi from peril. The sight of his friend surrounded by three thugs made him think of the fateful day on the beach from his childhood. Then he remembered Yamada on his knees, crying, in front of his wrecked store. Impulsively, without a word of warning, he

Face of a Stranger

grabbed Saigo's two men by their collars and tossed them against the wall; then he swept Saigo away from Takashi with a forearm to the chest, sending him to the floor.

The two other men picked themselves up, glanced at Kogoro and then at each other, then ran past Takashi and out the door. Saigo lay on the floor, his hand pressed against his sternum, gasping for breath.

Takashi stared at the farmer, amazed, while Kogoro gaped at Saigo with equal wonder at his own handiwork. "Why did you do that?" Takashi asked.

Kogoro blanched: was his premonition wrong? "Oh, but I . . . "

Shrieks of pain and anger startled them both. They turned to see Mrs. Inada thrashing poor Junzo with the rug beater while Inada tried vainly to call her off.

"Frighten a defenseless woman, will you? Send your lackeys to kidnap a young girl, will you? Extort our hard-earned money from us, will you? Shame on you! You're a disgrace!" she railed, swinging away.

"Help, help! Saigo! Uncle! Help! Murder! Mother!" Junzo cried, cowering, trying to ward off the mad woman's blows.

"Sumiko! Sumiko! This won't do! Live by the sword, die by the sword, remember?" Inada shouted helplessly.

Another one of Kato's men staggered in, his face and clothes smeared with soot. "Saigo! There you are! The boss sent me to find you!"

Mrs. Inada stayed her assault; Junzo slid to the floor, whimpering and rubbing his crown. Saigo, grimacing, pulled himself to his feet and panted wearily: "What is it now?"

Yoji Yamaguchi

"Come quick! We're in the shit now!"

"What d'ya mean?"

"They're burning us out like rats in a barn!"

"What?"

"They burnt down China Alley—and now they're heading for the gambling room and the restaurant!"

"Who?"

"Looks like everybody—the whole fucking town! C'mon!" He ran out the door.

Saigo hobbled out after him. Junzo jumped to his feet and ran after them, wailing: "My uncle! Where's my uncle?"

Moments after they left, the door opened again: it was Tsushida, hopping with excitement. "Oh glory be! The ruffians are routed! Kato's gang is fleeing town!"

"What?" Inada asked, astonished.

Tsushida said breathlessly: "The men who came here were sacking shops and beating innocent people all over town. So a group of townspeople gathered at Yamada's store and, led by Reverend Onara, Mrs. Hayashi, and Mrs. Urusaki, marched on the prostitutes' quarter. They evicted the women from the huts and began to demonstrate against Kato's latest outrage. Apparently, someone knocked over a lamp in the course of dismantling one of the huts, setting it on fire. The blaze inspired the crowd, and soon all of the huts were lit. A few of Kato's men arrived on the scene and tried to put them out, but the crowd fell upon them and they were forced to leave."

"Was anyone hurt?" Inada asked.

"None of the townspeople. As for Kato's gang, I don't know."

193

"What about the whore Kikue?" "What about Kikue?" Mrs. Inada and Takashi asked simultaneously. They glared at each other, and for a moment looked as if they were about to resume their confrontation. But Tsushida's news commanded their attention.

"I assume all the prostitutes escaped unharmed," he was saying. "In any case, they're all gone! And Kato and his men are next! The town will be free!" He skipped out the door happily. Inada and his wife looked at each other, then scurried out the door after him.

Takashi ran out the door as well, muttering in a distracted voice: "I have to find Kikue."

The lobby was empty. Kogoro wondered whether he had saved Takashi or not; his friend was more baffled than grateful when he pummeled his three would-be assailants. Kogoro blushed and broke out into a sweat, certain now that he had misconstrued matters, blundered into Takashi's business and ruined everything. As he debated whether or not to look for his friend amid the chaos, a voice coming from the top of the stairs startled him. "Pssst. Please help me, sir."

Kogoro looked up and nearly fell to his knees when he saw Hana, dressed in a simple blue kimono, her hair hanging luxuriantly over her shoulders. The likes of her beauty he had never seen before in his life; for a moment he wondered if she was human. His jaw sagged, and all he could do was stare dumbly.

She came galloping down the stairs with surprisingly loud steps even though barefooted, her hair bouncing, streaming behind her. In one hand she held a suitcase; in the other, a pair of wooden sandals.

When she reached the lobby she dropped her luggage at Kogoro's feet. "Help me: I've been kidnapped. These people are crazy; I don't know who they are or what they want. They got me out of that jail on that island, and now they say they're taking me to some place called *Montaanaa*. You know where that is?"

Kogoro shook his head, transfixed by Hana's beauty.

"Forget it! I'm not going to any nunnery. And I won't stay another minute in this place. I was better off in that prison cell. At least in there I didn't have to listen to this little fellow, Onara, and that huge woman, I forgot her name. What bores!"

Hana frowned. Kogoro was nearly catatonic; he hadn't moved an inch. "Are you listening? Are you all right?"

Kogoro replied with a barely perceptible nod.

"Good. Can you help me?"

He nodded again, with somewhat more vigor this time.

"Good. Now, how can we get out of here? I want to go far away, so they won't find me."

Kogoro's throat bobbed as he swallowed nervously; then he managed to croak: "I . . . have . . . a truck."

"*Truck?* An American *truck?*"

He nodded fearfully, as if he were no longer certain of the fact, simply because she sounded skeptical.

"Oh, I'm so glad I found you!" she exclaimed gratefully. Then she added: "Quickly, get the truck and bring it up to the hotel!"

195

Kogoro nodded frenetically, then bounded out the door like an eager dog.

Hana paced in circles with her arms crossed, her ears keen to any sound that might be her abductors returning. When she had her back partly turned to the door, a man stumbled in, catching her off guard. She whirled around, assuming it was Kogoro, and was about to rebuke him for dawdling and giving her a fright.

It was not him; it was Takashi Arai, panting heavily. His face was slick with sweat and his hair stuck out in all directions. He had a desperate gleam in his eyes. When he saw Hana he stopped in his tracks.

Hana backed a step away from the distracted-looking man, scanning the lobby for ways to escape. Where was that big bumpkin?

Takashi startled her again by bowing low and ostentatiously. "Ah, it's you. You're here! Welcome. Please excuse me for not meeting your boat . . . but, ah . . . the go-between seems to be missing . . . um, you see . . . we must leave here quickly . . . the owner is, ah . . . " His words came tumbling out, like marbles falling out of a sack.

"Who are you?" Hana demanded.

Takashi frowned, then grimaced and slapped his head. "Oh, of course . . . no picture . . . you don't recognize me," he muttered, almost to himself. He bowed again. "I am your husband," he declared.

"Husband?" Hana shrieked in surprise.

"Hai—Ara . . . er, Ichimon Nashitaro desu."

Yoji Yamaguchi

"'Penniless Boy?'" Hana burst out laughing. "I think there's been a mistake. I don't have a husband."

Takashi blinked like an idiot. "But . . . but . . . you are Kuruzaki Hana?"

"No. My name is Také, and I am not meant to be married by any man."

"I don't understand."

"Not even the Son of Heaven can marry me. Can't you tell I'm not of this earth?"

"Uhn?"

"I was born from a bamboo shoot that also spawned gold."

"Uhn?"

"*Amadera ni makase!*" she snapped, pointing a finger at him.

Kogoro appeared in the doorway, sweating profusely, his chest heaving like a bellows. In his own disorientation after meeting Hana, he could not find his truck and wound up running in circles before locating it.

"Ah, you're back at last!" Hana cried, relieved, as she rushed to Kogoro's side. She clutched his beefy arm and steered him between her and Takashi; then, standing on her toes, she whispered loudly in the direction of his ear, "This man is crazy, you know. He thinks we're supposed to be married. I have no idea who he is. He calls himself"—she giggled—"Ichimon Nashitaro."

Kogoro reddened with embarrassment at his friend's predicament. He wondered why Takashi was using a phony name and why he seemed so unlike himself. Hana's words—*This man is crazy . . . I have no idea who he is*—stunned him: she had no intention of marrying Arai, had no idea, even, who he was. Was he lying, then, trying to rob Kogoro of three hundred dollars? Kogoro could not believe it, seeing the desperate look on his friend's face.

Still, for reasons he could not understand himself, he suddenly did not want Arai to marry the beautiful girl; he realized he would do anything to prevent that from happening.

"Get me out of here, away from this guy!" Hana hissed. To Kogoro's ears, though, she might well have said "At thy foot I'll lay and follow thee my lord throughout the world."

Takashi, who had heard everything she said, held out his hands like a supplicant. "You know who I am. Don't you remember? The mansion? The forbidden rooms? How could you not know me?" Hana and Kogoro stared at each other. "I don't know what you're talking about," she said, fear rising in her voice.

Takashi fell to his knees. "I won't disappoint you again. I beg you to give me a second chance!"

"You really are mad!"

Takashi sprang to his feet and lunged at her, grabbing her by the shoulders. "I am your husband! We are meant to be together! You would not have come back to me otherwise!"

Hana screamed. "Help! Help!"

Instinctively, Kogoro wrapped his arm around Takashi's neck and flung him away; Takashi crashed his head against the wooden door and crumpled to the floor in a heap. Kogoro stared at him, horrified. Hana tugged at his arm and shouted, "Let's go!" Kogoro wanted to examine his friend more closely, but the girl kept pulling on his arm, surprising him with her strength.

He was even more surprised to see her sprinting barefoot to his truck, carrying the bulky suitcase as if it weighed nothing at all. "Come on! Come on! Don't go back!" she exhorted him; against his will, he obeyed. Her breathless voice was like a tether, pulling him behind her.

He overtook her and opened the passenger door for her. She handed him the suitcase, which was so much heavier than he expected that he nearly dropped it. Fortunately for them, he had left the engine idling, so they were able to speed off as soon as they both climbed in.

It was not a moment too soon, for Takashi came staggering out of the hotel, chasing after them. "Matte! Wait! You can't leave me like this! I am your husband! Come back!"

Hana watched Takashi recede from view and shuddered. Then the engine backfired, causing her to jump. "What was that?" she shrieked in alarm.

"Oh, uh, just the truck," Kogoro replied. "It does it all the time."

"It sounded like thunder—thunder from a clear blue sky." She looked at the massive fellow beside her, a bumpkin whose name she didn't even know: he was sweating profusely, and his larynx bobbed up and down nervously; his knuckles were white as he clutched the wheel as if to choke it to death. He was, without question, the ugliest man she had ever seen. And yet he had rescued her from the madman, no questions asked; something about him told her he was someone to whom one could entrust her life. "So, where are we going?" she asked.

• • •

Face of a Stranger

Takashi stood in the middle of the road, stunned, insensible. He did not even notice the bizarre sight approaching him: a woman in a white dress, her face covered by a lace veil. She walked up to him and announced herself: "Hajimemashite."

Takashi looked down at her with a start: the sight of the ghostlike figure made him gasp. When he recognized the dress as an American-style wedding dress, he thought it was Hana behind the veil. And yet he just saw her drive away with Doi—or did he? He backed away from the strange apparition. "Who are you?" he demanded.

"Kanai de gozaimasu," she replied sweetly.

"My wife?"

Slowly she lifted the veil from her face. It was Kikue.

"You?" he exclaimed. "What is this? What's going on? Why did Kuruzaki Hana run off with Doi? Why are you dressed like that? Is this a scam?"

"The scam I've pulled is the same one you pulled."

"What does that mean?"

She pulled from her sleeve a cracked and dog-eared photograph and handed it to him. It was the betrothal photo Oshichi had given her. "I don't understand," he said.

"Your name was Kimitake Hiraoka, though according to my friend Shino—who you met in the alley—it was Tsushima Shuji. You owned a dry goods store—though Shino says you were really a truck farmer—in Fremont, California; Anaheim, according to her. You were born in Wakayama and served in the army during the war with Russia. At least on those points we agree."

Takashi stared at her, dumb.

Yoji Yamaguchi

"By the way, I didn't know Kuruzaki Hana would be here; really you weren't supposed to see her, just as I was never supposed to see you."

Takashi stammered: "But . . . I don't understand. . . ."

"Neh, I have something else to show you." She produced a sheet of paper. He studied it. It was a list of names, each with a dollar figure next to it.

"What's this?"

"A list of my old debtors. I just sold their IOUs to Kato at quite a profit. If we were really getting married, I'd give them to you and we'd be rich. I'd say they're worth about five thousand dollars. . . ."

"F-f-five thousand?"

"Yes, that's two fortunes you've had slip through your fingers—both on the same day! Shikata ga nai, neh?" She turned and began to walk away. "Don't forget, you owe Doi three hundred dollars or two years," she called out.

"But . . . I gave that money to you!"

She stopped and turned around. "Iya, you gave it to a whore named Kikue, not me. That Kikue's dead and gone. You killed her."

"What? What are you talking about?"

"You killed her when you fell for her offer of a perfect bride. But you had help, too. If these Christians hadn't turned on her, I wouldn't be here now. Kikue would still be Kikue."

"Who are you?"

"Someone you'll never know," she said and turned away.

"Wait."

She stopped, her back still to him.

"Would you . . . ah . . . do you think . . . "

"Yes?"

"Could you lend me three hundred dollars?"

She looked over her shoulder. "Oh, no, I'm out of that business, too. I'm leaving town with my friend. Abayo, Baka-chan."

Long after she had turned the corner and disappeared from view, Takashi stared hard at the photo he was still holding. It was a poor likeness: unfocused and overexposed, the face barely discernible. The print was cracked and badly faded. He knew now what her scam was all about, as he touched his cheek, the bridge of his nose. Then he noticed something odd.

A mole above the right eyebrow—or was it a speck of dirt, a stain? He looked closer. There was no doubt: it was a mole. He rubbed his brow lightly. Then he dropped the photo and ran after Kikue, yelling:

"Hey! Wait! You made a mistake! This isn't my picture! This is somebody else! You confused me with somebody else!"

Yoji Yamaguchi